GAtsBy's PaRty

PATTI WHITE

GATSBY'S PARTY

THE SYSTEM AND

THE LIST IN

CONTEMPORARY

NARRATIVE

PURDUE UNIVERSITY PRESS
WEST LAFAYETTE, INDIANA

Printed in the United States of America

Book and jacket design by Susan Miller

Library of Congress Cataloging-in-Publication Data

White, Patti, 1951–
    Gatsby's party : the system and the list in contemporary narrative / by Patti White.
        p.   cm.
    Includes bibliographical references and index.
    ISBN 1-55753-020-3
    1. American fiction—20th century—History and criticism.
2. Lists in literature. 3. Fitzgerald, F. Scott (Francis Scott), 1896–1940. Great Gatsby. 4. English fiction—20th century—History and criticism. 5. System theory in literature. 6. Narration (Rhetoric) I. Title.
PS374.L52W47 1992
813'.509—dc20   91-47141
                                                                  CIP

Contents

Acknowledgments

WEST: Hal and Cathy White.

MIDWEST: Mary Sims.

EAST: Gerhard Joseph,
David Gordon, and
David Greetham.
Lynn Kadison.
Speed Hill,
Bill Kelly,
Joe Wittreich, and
Martin Stevens.
Mary Ann Caws.

chapter 1

Gatsby's Party

Relationality equals morphology.

—*Paul Young*
The Nature of Information

I know a man who once spent a summer memorizing the list of guests at Jay Gatsby's party. The reader can no doubt imagine the processes involved in such an endeavor: the excision of the list from its narrative surroundings; the copying and recopying of names; the formation of memory chunks and visual links between items; and the eventual recitation of the entire list at some late-summer academic cocktail party, perhaps with an accompanying explication of either the significance of the list in *The Great Gatsby* or of the memorization process itself. The man eventually forgot the names and lost the list in the recesses of memory, but he quite naturally still tells the story of that summer. Curiously, his tale would initially seem to suggest that his involvement with the list ceased when he could no longer recall its members. On the contrary, however, his position in regard to that list is as secure as it was during that cocktail-washed moment of triumph so long ago; the consistency of the relation between list and man is marked (and perpetuated by) his continual reactivation as a structural component in a complex information system surrounding *The Great Gatsby*.

The list in his narration is no longer the precise textual unit extracted from *Gatsby;* rather, it is a representation of that list, an invocation of the structural node formerly occupied by the complete list. However, the information system set up during the course of that long, hot summer is relatively unchanged: the list (even as mere notation) is still being transferred from the man to an audience. The formal relations between man and list have been maintained over the years—with no loss of coherence or systemic power. In addition, the list itself has maintained coherence: it still has informative value as performance, as a comment upon knowledge, and as a connection to the larger system surrounding *Gatsby.*

Relation is what determines not only the original structuration of the full guest list but also the list's participation in a series of systemic incarnations. As a part of the *Gatsby* system, it has narratological functions dedicated to the realization of an overall narrative strategy. And although the anecdote above gives the impression that the list was somehow captured while held in suspension within the textual artifact, that it was indeed captured and *removed,* the excision is merely metaphorical; the list maintains its functional position within the *Gatsby* narrative system while simultaneously occupying a position in the tangential system that coalesces around the act of memorization. The relations established between the list and the man make it a component in two separate but interacting systems.

The list also participates in an extranarratological temporal system. In one relational configuration, the list organizes time because it provides a structure for the amorphous academic summer confronting the man; in another, it functions as a time drain, a node to which limited temporal resources must be budgeted in competition with other demands in the man's temporal economy. Being ambirelational makes the list ambientropic. In the first configuration, the list reduces the entropic trend of academic summers toward disorganized lethargy; it actually makes time by providing a means of differentiation. In the second, the list is itself entropic, causing an expenditure of time and a resultant loss of time energy: an increase of entropy in a time-poor universe.

At the cocktail party, the Gatsby list maintains relations in at least four information systems: (1) in the narrative about memorization, the recitation of the list marks the successful conclusion of the quest—it is a monitoring device against which success can be measured; (2) in the social system, the list is an information channel for messages about intellectual competence, academic eccentricity, and/or appropriate party behavior; (3) in the literary system, the repetition of the Gatsby list continues an ongoing debate about the significance of the guest list to the *Gatsby* narrative; and (4) in the cultural system, the presentation of the list as a conceptual construct participates in discourses of cognition and epistemology.

The adventures of the Gatsby list are all made possible by—indeed, all constructed by—networks of relations. Relations between components, and relations between relational systems, seem to me simultaneously to identify and construct the conceptual world of narrative. These relations—difference, pattern, contiguity, coherence—in dynamic actualization are systems that produce space and structure in the literary universe.[1] Under analysis, a narrative reveals itself as a system of systems.

This system of systems—the infodynamic, textiform supersystem we know as narrative—works to create and perpetuate itself at the same time as it reduces the amount of unstructured information in the universe. As an information structure, it carries on both intrasystemic and extrasystemic communication, ordering time and space within and around it as it does so. Gregory Bateson suggests that the "essence and *raison d'être* of communication is the creation of redundancy, meaning, pattern, predictability, information, and/or the reduction of the random by 'restraint'" (1972, 132). Narrative systems do indeed function in precisely this way to foster informative interaction and limit the deleterious effects of noise and chaos, depending upon recognizable systemic operations to carry out these tasks.

In fact, the narrative "system" is a supersystem, a union of relatively autonomous systems that interact in the creation of the conceptual construct "narrative." Each system in the union

interacts horizontally and vertically with other systemic entities, and each is relationally constituted and relationally constitutive at the same time. In this figuration of narrative, the list
is a systemic component that is itself constructed by operations
functionally identical to those operative at the supersystemic
level; in this figuration, the list *is* the narrative in a structurally profound and systemically elegant sense.

A word about the selection of texts. As a work of criticism
focused on list structures, *Gatsby's Party* implicitly acknowl-
edges all participants in the listing tradition and naturally stands
indebted to the work of such great list makers as Joyce, Sterne,
Rabelais, and Homer. However, my concern here has been to
find lists which exemplify particular acts of structuration; these
lists enable a discussion of systemic operations, pattern recognition, list construction, and discourse formation within a context of literary interpretation. The four works included provide
a field of investigation and permit me to focus on list systems
in contemporary fiction as a practical application of a systems-
theoretical methodology; F. Scott Fitzgerald's list of guests from
The Great Gatsby serves as the frame and impetus for this
analysis of structural operations within narrative.

The first chapter introduces the reader to problems surrounding the list of guests at Gatsby's party and to the concept
of narrative as system. Chapter 2, "Toxic Textual Events," is
a systems-theoretical interpretation of Don DeLillo's *White
Noise,* focusing on DeLillo's use of the three-word list as
a narrative device, as well as his figuration of a multiscalar
narrative structure. This concrete and practical encounter
with narrative systems prepares the reader for a more theoretical approach to "system" in the next chapter.

"The Narrative Supersystem" is an overview of systemic construction and operation and an application of systems
theory to the functioning of narrative. Here, I return to
Gatsby as an exemplar of a typical narrative system. In chapter 4, "Surprise Roast," systems theory provides an entry into
Thomas Pynchon's *Gravity's Rainbow,* permitting an interpre-

tation based upon an analysis of systemic assertions of coherence and of Pynchon's use of patterned structures for narrative (and character) movement. Then, in "Patterns Within Patterns," I conduct an in-depth examination of pattern construction and recognition, making applications of patterning theory to narrative structuration and to the organization and functioning of the Gatsby guest list.

Chapter 6, "Two Hundred Whores," is a list-centered examination of John Barth's *The Sot-Weed Factor,* focusing on list-formation issues such as determination of sufficiency, the problem of excess, reading and construction strategies, and border permeability. The following section, "Inside the List," offers a consideration of classification and categorization and a discussion of the ways in which the Gatsby guest list reflects classificatory strategies and foregrounds certain problems inherent in the ordering of information.

Chapter 8, "Stuffed Parrots," is an interpretation of Julian Barnes's *Flaubert's Parrot* which finds mutually constitutive operations at work in the narrative structure of the novel and the ordering systems (the encyclopedia and the museum) chosen by narrator Geoffrey Braithwaite. "The Cultural Hypersystem" moves away from the previous chapter's consideration of a cultural discourse which enables the construction of entities such as the encyclopedia and the museum to focus on cultural discourse formation as a (sometimes chaotic) system that must both inhibit and encourage disorder as a means toward change. Here, Gatsby's guest list is viewed as an active participant in and mirror of this discourse—and as a potentially chaotic Baudrillardian hyperspace. Then, in "Gatsby's Party Revisited," Gatsby's funeral offers a final opportunity for a consideration of the guest list as a narratological (and systemic) structure and for final words on the problem of presence and absence.

Toxic Textual Events

The universe is a very unstable place; star systems collapse, elements decay, whole galaxies move in a mad dash toward the edge of reality. This instability has for some time been considered evidence of cosmic entropy, a dispersal of energy across the system and a sign of the ultimate decomposition of all structures into chaos. Lately, however, there seems to be some question about the inevitability of this process, some indication that the second law of thermodynamics has only local, rather than universal, relevance. The new physics suggests that entropy is not a completely linear process, that especially in "metaphorical" interpretations of the second law the increasing disorderliness of the universe is really a generative chaos which makes new structures possible and ensures that "complexity flourishes" (Gleick 1987, 308).

Chaos theory suggests that it is possible to decipher disorder, to read against disruption, and to restructure randomized information into coherent messages. Chaos, whether existing at the beginning of an ordering process or appearing at the end of a systemic collapse, represents the element pool from which new structures may be constructed; thus one reading of chaos results in a narrative of potential. Chaos also implies a narrative of differentiation: until it registers a tendency toward new periodic patterns or a predictable restabilization, the chaos outside whatever remains stable serves as a boundary between itself and the structure. And when the entropic system does at last move again toward structure, the elements not entering into order narrate the intervention of an ordering impulse: a Derridean trace, a significant absence, signals the presence of systematic intent.

A reading of this complexity, an analysis of new structures and of the forces of chaos, must naturally be conducted on a metasystemic level; from inside, entropic movement toward chaos continues to disrupt and impede the functioning of the system.[1] Within the system, accounts of local entropy would likely dominate any narrative of systemic movement through chaos toward some final state.[2] Consequently, in thermodynamics an intrasystemic narrative concentrates on heat loss; in linguistics, the narrative tracks an increase of disruptive and subversive noise.[3]

DeLillo's 1985 novel *White Noise* is, on one level, an intrasystemic narrative of entropic movement, an account of the disruptive effect of noise. Here, trapped in a decaying information structure, his characters struggle with the American mystery, trying to decipher their own lives while contending with increasing amounts of floating data. On another level, the novel is a metasystemic restructuring of chaos, a recycling of precisely those dispersed and disordered elements which the characters experience as noise.

Narrator Jack Gladney mirrors the novel's metasystemic restructuring of chaos when he attempts a narrativization of his own family's refuse. Searching for evidence of his wife's drug habit, he opens his trash compactor and tries to read his family's refuse as a system of signs leading to a discovery of "habits, fetishes, addictions, [and] inclinations" (259). What he finds inside is a collection of elements which have fallen out of the domestic system; they are waste products, discarded information, household noise:

> a horrible clotted mass of hair, soap, ear swabs,
> crushed roaches, flip-top rings, sterile pads
> smeared with pus and bacon fat, strands of
> frayed dental floss, fragments of ballpoint refills,
> toothpicks still displaying bits of impaled food
> [and] a pair of shredded undershorts with lipstick
> markings. . . . (259)

Outside their compactor, these items are message fragments, no longer communicative because they have lost their contexts. Like loose particles in a reordered universe, they tell only the story of a withdrawn presence as they signal their availability for organization into order. Gladney, unable to perceive the potential for a construction of new messages, attempts to replace these items in their lost contexts; however, the waste retains its status as noise and resists Gladney's efforts at recuperation. His failure suggests that any reverse reading of chaos must be highly speculative and ultimately uninformative.

The construction of *White Noise* foregrounds the problem Jack Gladney faces: how to make sense out of the millions of fragmented messages now compacted into the waste system of American culture. DeLillo, having a deeper understanding of chaos than his narrator, makes no attempt at recuperation of lost contexts; instead, he forces discarded particles into newly informative arrangements, using noise as the building blocks of narrative. He seems to suggest that a program of recycling may be the only way to manage the astounding noise level of the information age, the only way to clear the system of disruptive waste. Obviously unable to read the chaos of culture on a meta-systemic level, he tries to offer an intrasystemic solution, offering *White Noise* as a model of noise management, a hedge against the onset of entropy in what he clearly perceives as a declining system.

Recent systems theories have suggested that the structure of natural and social systems implies a designated facility for the processing and exchange of information. These theories define systems by the ways in which information is generated, collected, and exchanged; further, they locate systemic health in noise-free communication.[4] Systems analysts point to the DNA genetic code, which ensures its own replicability, has redundancy rules to guarantee accurate transmission, and can incorporate novel messages by means of self-corrective structural change, as a model information system; noise enters this system as mutation, but even then the system is likely to meet its goals.[5] Language-based systems have similar operative structures that enable transference of messages, limit unpredictability, and reduce the interference of noise. However, none of these operations can ensure the eradication of noise; once generated, it may remain free within the system, disrupting further communication.

A system which has declined from a noise-free state to one of pervasive clamor may cease to function; since information exchange is essential for motive power, extreme difficulty in transmission may simply halt all processes. In an infosystem, noise is correlated with random message production. This is so because in noisy, or highly entropic, systems, there is "no reason to expect . . . one particular arrangement [of elements] over any of the colossal number of other possible arrangements" (Campbell 1982, 46); in other words, any moment of stabilization is equally likely to result in nonsense or information. Such a system produces "messages" that do not communicate, and it cannot predictably perform a goal-directed exchange of information. Like the Gladney's trash compactor, an entropic system produces uncommunicative chaos.

This movement toward chaos seems to confirm the fears of those who have seen access to information as a threat to the stability of society and even of the human psyche. As early as 1800, William Wordsworth was concerned about the effect of the proliferation of information on the human brain. In his "Preface" to the second edition of *Lyrical Ballads*, he decried the "degrading thirst for outrageous stimulation" needed to excite brains deadened by modern times; he warned that

> a multitude of causes, unknown to former times,
> are now acting with combined force to blunt the
> discriminating powers of the mind, and, unfitting
> it for all voluntary exertion, to reduce it to a state
> of almost savage torpor. (1965, 249)

Chaotic uncommunicability and overstimulation both lead to the "savage torpor" Wordsworth describes. Randomly produced messages eventually result in a frustrated refusal of the "addressee" role; if a message is contra-contextual there is no motivation for the addressee to play his part: no interpretation of, response to, or transfer of the message is likely to be appropriate, and this node in the informational system is blocked. An effect similar to this blockage occurs when an overstimulated brain, having reacted with equivalent intensity to all manner of stimuli, begins either to flatten meaning or to flatten response: in either case, there is a decline in acknowledgment of information content and, eventually, an inability to respond at all.

For a rather mundane example of this effect, one might consider how the noise of a whirring fan will, in a relatively short time, recede from consciousness. The movement of the fan blades produces a rhythmic noise that has only one message: "on." Once that message has been conveyed, repetitions of the messages are, according to information theory, simply "noise": containing no novel content, interfering with the reception of other messages by virtue of the attention they require. In an effort to protect itself, the brain blocks awareness of the sound—in this case, a beneficial overload response. However, when faced with continual overstimulation, the system's capacity for noise reduction may be exhausted; now the brain may lose the ability to discriminate between "noise" and "information" or it may refuse to respond to any outside stimulation and thus inhibit further information processing—perhaps even endangering systemic well-being.[6]

A common term for undifferentiated background noise is the one DeLillo uses as his title: white noise.[7] Here, noise is linked with a word that has ambiguous signification; whiteness can imply innocence and availability, or it can threaten blankness, suggesting a ground where the ability to discriminate has been lost.[8] In *White Noise,* the characters encounter whiteness and noise in many forms, but they are finally unable to reconcile the ambiguity the title suggests. Further, the tendency of information to *become* noise complicates their attempts to distinguish one from the other, and so they discover that their attempts at message transference and systematization of knowledge are·hampered by a failure of boundary definition. In the end, these characters are so bludgeoned by their encounters with nonsense that they look upon supermarket tabloids as providers of "everything that we need that is not food or love" (326). No longer able to discriminate between noise and information, the characters fall into a torpor of acceptance, looking for messages from the dead in the "waves and radiation" that pervade American life.

Waves of light and sound inform the narrative structure of *White Noise;* the effect of DeLillo's construction is at once visual and aural, cinematic (perhaps telematic) and sonic. Appealing to the reader's knowledge of several subgenres (the academic novel, the disaster movie, the detective story), *White Noise* in its very structure seems to imitate the condition of overload that DeLillo warns against. Indeed, the story line is even interrupted by what, on a structural level, may be analogous to commercials and deliveries of junk mail: three-word lists that name products, an announcement from Waveform Dynamics listing the twelve necessary steps for proper payment of bills, a generic listing of Cable TV offerings.

Jack Gladney is completely conscious of the waves and radiations that constitute the substructure of his narrative. The noise of American culture—the waste product of the information age—forms an aharmonic score beneath his record: the susurration of tires upon the freeway, the omnipresent voice of the television, the hiss of the supermarket doors. These sounds, soothing to Jack as background noise, become menacing or fatiguing when they are brought into conflict with his attempts to gain or interpret information. He understands that continuous noise has a tendency to flatten meaning, and the threatened blankness dismays him.

Gladney clearly fears lack of distinction, especially the loss of order implied in death. The implications are instantly clear to him when his wife Babette wonders "What if death is nothing but sound? . . . You hear it forever. Sound all around. How awful" (198). His response, "Uniform, white," emphasizes the undifferentiated nature of white noise, the lack of borders between sounds; such randomness, such a failure of order, is precisely what Gladney fears in death: dissolution, loss of individuality, the inability to make his death distinct from the deaths of others. When he finally identifies the voices of the dead in the waves and radiation of the supermarket, they are the dead speaking as a whole, from within the white world of chaotic sound: no one voice stands out from the others.

As the voice of the narrator, of course, Gladney's voice does have primacy and distinction. In a first-person narration styled as recollection, the event in *White Noise* are reported to us from some unidentified point in the future.[9] No other voice is recorded as narrator although there is some question about the source of the pervasive three-word lists; because Gladney makes no claim to them, these are at least potentially anonymous, and thus potentially outside his control.

If they are not spoken in Gladney's voice, the lists (which read like the incantations of a materialist religion) are at least in a voice *like* Gladney's. LeClair points out that these lists are indeed characteristic of Gladney's style, for he often thinks in groups of three. However, LeClair inclines to the possibility that Gladney has lost control of his narrative, that the lists may come from outside Gladney's consciousness and may thus simply be "part of the circumambient noise in which he exists . . ." (1987, 211).

This inclination leads to interesting possibilities. If they are nonconscious intrusions of "circumambient noise," the lists are textual representations of Jack's own experiences with noise; their presence would then mean that he has finally been unable to filter out the noise he combats throughout the course of the novel. On the other hand, it may be that these lists are indeed products of Gladney's brain but that he has no conscious control over their construction and placement. In this case, the lists may be symptomatic of a nervous-system disorder—perhaps the first sign of the "nebulous mass" which Gladney believes is growing inside him as a result of his exposure to toxic material.

On a metasystemic level one might consider these lists a sort of narrative toxin: nonorganic substances intruding into an organic system and disrupting the flow of information through it. Consider, as analogy, the result of Jack Gladney's exposure to Nyodene Derivative. Gladney, informed that the toxin has made its way into his system, is forced to reevaluate his life in the face of this knowledge; the reader, confronted with one of these lists, is forced to reevaluate the course of the narrative. An encounter with "Krylon, Rust-Oleum, Red Devil" (159) or "Dacron, Orlon, Lycra Spandex" (52) in an otherwise linear and logical narrative structure clearly calls for heightened attention. The reader is now forced to process and eventually bypass these bits of "meaningless" noise which have lodged themselves between contiguous sections of narrative. Further, the reader's own information pool has been tainted by these packets of words; meaningful or not, they are now located in memory and cannot be flushed out.

In effect, the lists are inevitably meaningful. Under analysis, all bits of data (whether finally labeled "noise" or "information") acquire significance by virtue of their roles within the system. Information serves to power the system; noise blocks or delays systemic processes. An examination of the three-word [trilog] lists suggests three possible functions.[10] One, as intrusions (either environmental or unconscious) into Gladney's narrative, they mark a breakdown in either the noise-reduction processes or the information-transference processes of the system, thus signifying the state of the system. Two, as part of a strategy of toxicity, they are intrusions into the contiguity of the narrative structure and are designed to force the reader into noise-reduction strategies; as such, they provide information about the state of the narrative and its vulnerability to disruption. Three, as constituents of narrative, they carry the story forward and/or comment upon the progress and structure of the tale; in this case, the strategy may be looked upon as being either intra- or extrasystemic since the authority of these lists is in question.

LeClair offers one other suggestion: he sees DeLillo's trilog lists as mirrors of the novel's tripartite structure (1987, 211). It seems to me, however, more likely that the lists in fact serve simultaneous functions: as noise, disrupting the narrative and problematizing the narrative situation, *and* as information, capable of being read within the context of the surrounding episode and at the same time modeling for the reader a metasystemic recycling program that turns noise into narrative.

For instance, a list of credit cards ("MasterCard, Visa, American Express" [100]) bisects one of the novel's many discussions about death. In this case, Jack Gladney and Babette are concerned about who will die first and how the survivor will be able to cope with the loss. Just before the list intervenes, Babette claims that she and Jack are safe from death "as long as there are dependent children in the house." The list, in its immediate context, points out that Babette's notion constitutes a sort of living-on-credit: she counts upon having the term of her life extended to meet the needs of the children. In addition, the list introduces a connection between life and credit that will reappear when colleague Murray Siskind tells Jack that killing extends life: he says that the "more people you kill, the more credit you store up" (290) as a defense against your own death.

Just after the intervention of the list, Jack claims that he wants to die first. Because the presence of the list seems to require heightened attention, an alert reader may later recall it when the claims of both Jack and Babette are proved wrong. Not long after this scene, Babette's safety net fails to hold: Jack is exposed to highly toxic Nyodene D not only while the children are still dependent, but actually in the act of saving the children from the threat of death. This exposure seems to grant Jack's extremely rash wish—he is virtually assured an early death. However, once faced with his own mortality, he becomes desperate to outlive the entire family.

Foreknowledge of death is, of course, a definitive human condition. But even as they try to escape the fear this knowledge generates, Jack and Babette are forced to recognize that "all plots move in one direction" (199), toward death. In the midst of this realization, a list of gasolines, "Leaded, unleaded, super unleaded," seems to comment upon motive force and forward motion, linking fossil fuels to the drives that power human endeavors. Just before the list, Gladney's narrative recounts the small intimate movements, the minute adjustments, involved in a prolonged embrace with his wife:

> How subtly we shifted emotions, found shadings,
> using the scantest movement of our arms, our
> loins, the slightest intake of breath, to reach
> agreement on our fear, to advance our competi-
> tion, to assert our root desires against the chaos
> in our souls. (199)

These movements, powered by fear and love, are then contrasted against the brute force of the automobile, which is powered by controlled explosions.[11]

This particular list seems to comment upon motive and motion; it also marks a discussion which, while focusing on an attempt to block movement, precipitates Jack's movement toward the climactic scene of the novel. The moment Jack recounts above leads to intercourse, and afterward Jack and Babette begin to discuss Babette's experiment with Dylar. Ironically, this drug is specifically designed to inhibit movement in the brain—it blocks the admission of electrical impulses to the neural receptors that register fear of death. The drug has not been successful; Babette still fears death. Consequently, her plot must continue to move in a forward direction, toward death, and this is exactly where Jack's reception of Babette's story eventually leads him. Driven by jealousy and envy, he goes to Iron City to kill the man who gave Babette drugs in exchange for sexual favors.

The noise level of the novel is very intense by the time Jack Gladney begins his attack on Babette's "Mr. Gray." The narrative has by now been interrupted seven times by the ambiguous trilog lists. In addition, many other sorts of narrative structures have managed to insert themselves into Jack's narration: tabloid news stories; survivors' tales; bits of radio and television shows; sirens and evacuation directions; a recitation of cold remedies; supermarket parking violation announcements. All of these, the residue of Jack's visual and aural environment, have been swept up into his own narrative; preserved in his story, they exist in a sort of narrative limbo, no longer attached to their supposed contexts: they are now "noise." As narrator, Gladney is performing a masterful juggling act, keeping all these bits of information afloat; as character in his own narrative, Gladney is nearing the point of overload.

A systemic breakdown is precisely what Jack Gladney faces when he finally tracks down "Mr. Gray": Willie Mink, the mysterious supplier of Dylar. Addicted to his own fear suppressant, Mink is already subject to some of the side effects he warned Babette against. Before her agreement to test the drug was finalized, Mink informed Babette that use of the drug could result in brain death, loss of motor function, an inability to "distinguish words from things," and perhaps even death (193). When Gladney finds Mink, who has hidden himself in a motel in Iron City, he discovers that Mink can no longer discriminate between language and reality and is subject to uncontrollable repetitions of phrases and sentences that have entered his memory via the air waves.

Jack uses Mink's disability as a weapon; calling out "plunging airplane," he is amused to see Mink assume the proper crash position (309). Later, while Mink crawls into the bathroom to avoid the impact of Gladney's words, Jack whispers "hail of bullets" and then "fusillade" in a sort of linguistic preview of the gun battle that is about to take place (311).

This confusion of word with referent is prepared for by still another three-word list, one that intrudes into Gladney's narrative as he recounts the journey toward Iron City and the showdown with Mink. This list is comprised of full phrases substituting for their now common acronyms: "Random Access Memory, Acquired Immune Deficiency Syndrome, Mutual Assured Destruction" (303). Although the phrases reveal their full meaning when the acronyms are expanded into words, the list is revelatory only in retrospect: once the outcome of the scene with Mink is revealed, an act of contraction pulls the narrative (and the reader) back into the list that precedes it. Upon review, the phrases now seem to label Mink's dementia (random access of memory), comment upon the contamination of Mink's language processes by reality confusion (essentially an acquired loss of our natural immunity to this disorder), and predict the mutual attempts at destruction to come (in which Jack shoots Mink and Mink shoots Jack and neither, ironically, dies).

Gladney hopes that his assault on Mink will restore his own life force; Murray has told him that "to kill . . . is to gain life-credit" (290). Now labeled a "dier" in his hospital test records, Jack is determined to renew his membership in the rolls of the living. In addition, the assault will punish Mink for the theft of Babette's sexual energy while giving Jack access to whatever supply of Dylar Mink may have secreted with him at the motel.

Jack has a plan of action, which he repeats (expanding it each time) in an incantatory fashion, as if he could, by speaking, effect the carrying out of his design. This incantation instills in him a sense of inevitability, creates an exquisite assurance that is not broken until the plan literally explodes in his face. When the moment for action comes, he fails to carry out the plan precisely enough to ensure its success; rather than firing all three of the bullets at Mink, he leaves one bullet in the gun when he places it in Mink's hand in simulation of suicide.

The bullet that Mink fires at Jack releases him from the spell the incantation creates; in that trance, Jack (having overloaded his noise-reduction capacity by attending to his own repeated messages) perceives noise in all its sensory glory—acutely articulated, densely textured, visually and aurally elegant. His senses are so highly stimulated that he finds "extra dimensions [and] super perceptions" everywhere; however, when Mink's bullet hits home, Jack's pain reduces the heightened perceptions to "visual clutter, a whirling miscellany, meaningless" (313).

The noise value, the "whiteness" of the "whirling miscellany," is made relatively clear throughout the scene. Before he is bemused by his incantation, Jack observes that there is "white noise everywhere" (310): as he waits for Mink to come out of his crash position, he notices that the television picture has become jumpy, wobbly, and snarled and that the air of the room is "busy" (310). However, his ability to discriminate between information and white noise is soon lost.

Having discussed his own whiteness with Mink ("it's because I'm dying"), Jack pursues Mink into the white bathroom, where he notices that there is "sound all around"; because his processing capacity is overloaded, he fails to connect this with Babette's earlier concern that white noise might be the sound of eternity (198). Instead, he reads the noise as a "network of meanings" (312) converging to grant him identity. Vision and sound blur into whiteness around him: Mink's face becomes a "white buzz" as he cowers by the toilet, desperately ingesting white Dylar tablets; the sound of the gunshot "snowballs" around the room.

For Jack, the assault has been a sensory extravaganza. He has seen and heard intensely, with a recognition of differences in frequency and wavelength, with an acknowledgment of luminance and purity (312). However, since Jack has turned his attention to the data themselves, to their waves and radiations, the structure containing them has become invisible: the message has decomposed into noise.

The danger of the white noise in this scene is masked by the sort of reductionism suggested earlier by Jack's wife. Babette, a specialist in popular versions of adult education,[12] believes that "a person can change a harmful condition" by reducing it to its parts; she wants to "make lists, invent categories, devise charts and graphs" (191) in order to understand

and control threateningly complex situations. However, a greater attention to detail is fatal to Jack's plan, causing him to forget that the gun contains *three* bullets, not two. Further, his absorption in the beauty of the sensory context distracts Jack from the content of the messages: terror, submission, pain. This information about Mink's condition calls for a response from Jack that is not forthcoming until his own pain reduces "those vivid textures and connections" to "mounds of ordinary stuff" (313).

The competition between detail and structure is a difficult one for the characters in *White Noise* to resolve. Their brains are constantly called away from goal-seeking tasks to process the random bits of information that settle into consciousness out of the air waves. A general malaise, an uneasiness in the presence of overwhelming data, is expressed; there is simply too much to know, too many kinds of information to keep track of. When Babette is faced with Heinrich's command of technological and statistical data about magnetic fields, she laments the loss of the old knowledge: "Is this what they teach in school today? What happened to civics . . . ?" (176). In response to this loss, she tries to retrieve her school-day knowledge base by means of data recollection:"Latvia, Estonia and Lithuania . . . Angles, Saxons and Jutes." For her, memory is access to facts, rote recall of information bits from a pool of safe, predictable data. Her tendency to group data into logically linked chunks[13] is one of the natural mechanisms of recall, a sort of paradigmatic response to an internal game of "Trivial Pursuit." It is also a defense against the increasing complication of life in a world where "all these shifting facts and attitudes . . . just started appearing" (171).

For Babette, list making is a coping mechanism that can help her organize the "mounds of ordinary stuff" that make up daily life.[14] In her desire for order, she resembles the shoppers at the supermarket who consult lists that guide them through the labyrinth of attractive data arrayed on the shelves (326); both turn to the reductive or the prescriptive list as a weapon against chaos, a means of information fixation and control. An imposition of order, the list fixes information and makes it available for use; it can then serve as a basis for decision making, be a guide to action, or be transferred to another location. Further, as a stable structure, the list can be used as a screen or filter for processing other bodies of information. Jack moves toward this sort of filtering when he compiles a list of words that sound the same in both German and English (274) and then uses the list to construct an opening address for his Hitler conference. His impulse is a useful one; unfortunately, the template or redundancy rule he uses to control unpredictability severely limits the informative capacity of his new structure: his message ("command of German") barely gets through.

Because it is inherently limiting, because it reduces the capacity for innovative communication, list making is only ameliorative as a response to information anxiety.[15] Although it is a useful device for coping with the deluge of information we are subject to, it cannot, finally, restrict the tendency of information to slip out of message patterns and float free. Lists are too static, too dependent upon context, and too reflective of a specific process of construction to be useful over the long term; eventually, the data contained within lose their freshness, or the context changes so radically that the content loses its integrity. Lists, like the items in DeLillo's supermarket, have a limited shelf life.

Once a list is removed from its context, its movement toward the condition of noise accelerates. For instance, "The Airport Marriott, the Downtown Travelodge, the Sheraton Inn and Conference Center" (15) is encountered in the context of a discussion between Jack and Babette about where to put a visiting stepchild; here, it comments upon the difficulties of "modular" families as it points out the increasing modularity of the places Americans choose to stay.[16] Encountered elsewhere, the list still might comment upon the dull equivalence of these motels, but the reference to the problems of divorced and remarried parents whose children come and go would be lost.

The list is also dependent upon intrasystemic stability. The items that comprise the list lose their coherence if their relationship to each other changes: if the Marriott chain fails and closes, or if we include the Dew-drop Inn instead of the Travelodge, the internal integrity of the list is weakened. The message is noise free only as long as all original conditions of construction and selection prevail. As noise seeps into the exchange, the informative nature of the list, as well as its conservative function, changes.

Ironically, the most effective act of information conservation in *White Noise* takes place in the supermarket. This quintessentially American location[17] is, for all the characters in the novel, a three-dimensional list that both contains and conceals the "American mystery." For Murray Siskind, it is a place of spiritual replenishment, a fountain of "psychic data" (37).[18] For Jack Gladney, the supermarket represents the kind of fullness that Walt Whitman tried to convey in his catalogues and enumerations. He shops and wonders at

> the sheer plenitude those crowded bags suggested, the weight and size and number, the familiar package designs and vivid lettering, . . .
> [at] the sense of replenishment we felt, the sense of well-being, the security and contentment these products brought to some snug home in our souls. . . . (20)

Whitman recognized that concepts of diversity and plenitude were crucial to the construction of an American identity. His impulse toward enumeration, which can certainly be read as an act of praise and possession through naming, is also an appreciation of abundance; as such, it is an early sign of the particular drive toward surplus that often seems to characterize America—and surplus, an array of alternatives sufficient to satisfy and even exhaust demand, is what makes the supermarket possible.[19] Here, protected from outside interference, shoppers encounter the American message in nearly pure form: their participation shifts data in and through a structure that is essentially conservative, their presence asserts and affirms a message about national identity.

The American notion of plenitude, of material options, is closely bound to a self-image that encompasses and even glorifies a production chain: raw material, manufacture, and marketing are all implied in the presence of the product on the shelf. The significance of that presence is thus overdetermined; national stability and security, chemical and agricultural technology, commercial competition, and local determinations of product needs all bear upon the availability of any individual item. However, what makes the supermarket so rich in data is not only the presence of any individual item (something of a miracle in itself), but the presence of many representatives of relatively equivalent items, all competing for attention and ultimate selection.

The sense of well-being Jack Gladney experiences in the presence of loaded grocery carts thus comes partly from the safety represented by easily acquired sustenance, partly from his identification with the national experience, and partly from the closure represented in a successful negotiation of the psychic labyrinth of the supermarket itself. Having entered this labyrinth and emerged intact, Gladney has valiantly contended with, perhaps even deciphered, an overwhelmingly dense sensory environment.

The goods on the supermarket shelves, like the information floating on the air waves or the long lists of occupations in Whitman,[20] are virtually impossible to assimilate—numerous, diverse, attractive and repellent at the same time, they dazzle us with data. Gladney finds it compelling:

> The bins were arranged diagonally and backed
> by mirrors that people accidentally punched
> when reaching for fruit in the upper rows. . . .
> Apples and lemons tumbled in twos and threes
> when someone took a fruit from certain places in

the stacking array. There were six kinds of ap-
ples, there were exotic melons in several pastels.
Everything seemed to be in season, sprayed,
burnished, bright. (36)

Situated in a microcosm of America, a place that is democratic
and well-lit, these products make declarative statements about
the national condition while simultaneously stimulating the
brain to the point of overload.

This stimulation is itself, Gladney finds, peculiarly and tri-
umphantly American. During a conversation with scientist
Winnie Richards, he learns that what Winnie knows of the
human brain makes her "proud to be an American" because the
"infant's brain develops in response to stimuli [and we] still lead
the world in stimuli" (189). She sees American culture as a
positive force for growth and development; like Murray Siskind,
who moves through the supermarket fingering and sniffing
packages, she sees an abundance of data as a definitive American advantage.

However, what DeLillo suggests in his construction of the
supermarket as a location of sensory overstimulation is that an
abundance of data does not necessarily lead to an increase in
information. Although the supermarket contains a rich pool of
constituent elements, those elements can only be arranged in a
limited number of ways: there is little in the way of innovation
or surprise here. Consequently, the tendency is toward conservation of information rather than exchange; the information
does not go out of the system to affect other systems, the
repeated messages eventually elicit no response. The ultimate
effect of this conservation and repetition is either inattention
or breakdown.

Inattention has a deleterious effect, taking the brain out of
the message-production and processing mode and leaving it in
a passively receptive condition that will eventually overwhelm
the system with useless data.[21] But tuning out is not the only
harmful overload response; "tuning wrongly," the "wrong kind
of attentiveness," is equally perilous. Murray Siskind tells his

colleagues that an inappropriate response to data—one that privileges a commercial for "Automatic Dishwasher All" over "a forest fire on TV"—leads to "brain fade," a condition brought on by a misuse of and subsequent exhaustion of our data-collection capacities (67).

In a "world of hostile facts" (81), right attention is essential; otherwise, paralyzed by brain fade, we sink in the sea of floating noise. An intelligence dulled by constant overstimulation, a judgment hampered by a reversal of relative significance, is not prepared for the effort required in the recuperation of a world of "abandoned meanings" (184); further, this task cannot be undertaken by systems completely occupied by synchronous noise reduction and information processing. Reconstruction, a reordering of chaos, requires both capability and capacity, discrimination and time, to pick out the recyclable noise from the waste heap of discarded information.

Jack Gladney cleans house after he discusses his impending death with Murray Siskind. Enraged at the increasing toxification of his life, he finally reacts against the "things" that have gotten him into "this fix" (294). And since he is powerless against the major toxins in his world, he turns against the annoying clutter that informs his domestic life. Jack tries to strip down, to purify his life as a way to return to sense and perhaps prepare for death. As he does this, he creates a waste system very much like the one he encountered earlier in his search through the trash compactor. Ranging through the house, he discards

> picture-frame wire, metal book ends, cork coast-
> ers, plastic key tags, dusty bottles of Mercuro-
> chrome and Vaseline, crusted paintbrushes,
> caked shoe brushes, clotted correction fluid . . .
> candle stubs, laminated placemats, frayed pot
> holders . . . padded clothes hangers, the magnetic
> memo clip-boards, . . . diplomas, certificates,
> awards and citations . . . used bars of soap, damp
> towels, [and] shampoo bottles with streaked
> labels and missing caps. (294)

This household waste duplicates in domestic form the multiform cultural waste pervading the novel. These are items that have been retained in the house long after their usefulness has passed; this is physical white noise, the mundane litter that interferes with the maintenance of domestic coherence. Jack's solution is an extremely local one, however; his removal of the waste, though perhaps an effort of right attention, is in no way an eradication of it. The waste simply appears somewhere else, still noise, still chaotic. Jack is simply not able to step outside the system he is part of: he is not able to reconstruct, to bring order out of chaos.

Essentially, Jack is trapped inside the supermarket that is the source of many of the items he discards; the system he operates in is virtually finalized,[22] and there are no structures permitting rule change on his part.[23] At its best, the supermarket is a Whitman list gone wild, a paean to American abundance; at its worst, DeLillo seems to suggest, it is the sign and the source of uncontrolled and uncontrollable waste, an entropic system that ultimately produces noise and little else.

At the end of the novel, some perverse management decision causes the shelves at Gladney's supermarket to be rearranged and there is

> agitation and panic in the aisles, dismay in the
> faces of the older shoppers. They walk in a frag-
> mented trance, stop and go, clusters of well-
> dressed figures frozen in the aisles, trying to
> figure out the pattern, discern the underlying
> logic. . . . (325)

The internal coherence of the system has broken down, and because there is so much data to be made intelligible, so many packages and brands and colors and prices to be sorted, the exhausted and overstimulated shoppers cannot decipher the new code; they have seen formerly sense-bearing patterns dissolve into white noise before their eyes.

If America is indeed declining into a condition of white noise, DeLillo seems here to suggest that the continued viability of the system depends on a will and capacity for restructuring chaos. The novel is itself evidence that a program of recycling informational waste can be effective: the trilog lists—drawn from the noise of American culture—prove to be effective narrative bridges, capable of carrying themes and transporting action, just as indestructible plastic can be recycled, reformed, and used in construction.[24]

If no systemic solutions to chaos are attempted, then the only alternative may be to wait for the metasystem to regulate itself. Chaos theory suggests that fluctuations leading to new structures appear in the very midst of systemic breakdown; this reinterpretation of physics indicates that, eventually, new structures may coalesce out of the very chaos that now oppresses systemic vitality. In the meantime, local entropic movement toward undifferentiated noise will no doubt leave us all as confused as DeLillo's supermarket shoppers: disoriented, unable to decode the simplest messages, we will fall into the torpor Wordsworth predicted for us and must then pray that a holographic scanner at the check-out line will separate us from the data that surround us.

chapter 3

The Narrative Supersystem

*Cybernetics takes the view that the
structure of the machine or organism
is an index of the performance that
may be expected of it.*

—Norbert Wiener
The Human Use of Human Beings

A narrative system is a device for maintaining order in the face of encroaching chaos. This infodynamic organism differentiates itself from environmental or extrasystemic chaos by establishing structural and functional borders and controlling and processing the flow of information through its structures. In the course of this structuration, it maintains internal coherence by regulating the relations between its own components and minimizing the effects of both intrasystemic and extrasystemic turbulence. Should any system fail to perform these anti-chaotic functions, it would suffer loss of identity (since systemic identity depends upon particular sets of external and internal relations) and eventually face entropic dissolution: decaying internal processes would move it toward maximum predictability or toward information randomization, the informational equivalent of thermodynamic heat death.[1] Consequently, all purposive activity within the system moves in the direction of order, toward the maintenance of coherence and therefore toward the continuation of the system *as* system. All other systemic products are functions of this primary task.

A narrative system instantiates itself through ordering processes; the maintenance of relations between its substantive components not only creates it as both system and narrative, but systemic processes actually increase the amount of order in a particular region, thus reversing (locally) the entropic motion of the universe. However, when narrative systems work to increase structure in spite of their own entropic tendencies (diffusion of energy, transmission noise, fluctuation of component relations), this apparent defiance of the second law of thermodynamics merely signals an open systemic structure, not a collapse of the laws of physics. For open systems, maximum entropy is not an attractor state;[2] rather, such systems are able to utilize the movement of entropy across systemic borders to power their own structuration processes so that what might otherwise enter a system as a chaotic incursion can be channeled toward innovation and growth.

Thermodynamic configuration is defined by entropy flow. A closed system *contains* its increasing disorder; since none can escape, the entropy level must either remain constant or increase as systemic order breaks down. An open system has an inflow of negentropy (an increase in the level of energy, information, or order within the system) and a corresponding outflow of entropy (a loss of energy or information and an increase of disorder in the external world).[3] In other words, closed systems consume their own resources until differentiation becomes impossible and all activity finally subsides. Open systems, however, do exchange energy with the outside, and they use this energy to maintain internal functions without cannibalization of the system. Avoiding the equilibrium of maximum entropy, these systems use the fluctuation of entropic forces to perpetuate themselves as theoretically immortal processing and structuring entities.[4]

At a very basic level, a narrative can be described as an infodynamically open system, one that processes information through a text when an exchange is activated by a reader.[5] In this figuration, the narrative receives negentropy from the reader, and intratextual information is processed in response to (and by means of) that influx of power. The reader's investment of power in the system's processing functions naturally causes an increase of reader entropy; however, when negentropy flows back to the reader in the form of information (or narrative) energy, the situation is reversed. Now, the system suffers an increase in entropy and must seek further energy input. The narrative exhibits its vacant reader-energy position as evidence that it is available for reactivation—and every new reader/narrative exchange leaves the system in precisely this same, highly advantageous position. Since the narrative's systemic goal is the continual processing of reader energy through its text and the consequent instantiation of itself *as* narrative, its performance capacity is endless so long as it has access to this outside energy.

If the narrative system were closed, or isolated from its environment, it would be forced to end its operations as soon as its internal resources were consumed; for instance, once textual units had been regularized into specific configurations, the process of structuration would cease and block any further operation. However, we know that reader input, as well critical input, can alter the significatory relations of textual units even though the physical text itself is not rearranged. The processing of the text does not consume the text nor does it fix the conceptual construct we term "narrative" in a rigid form. Rather, the physical structure of the text is a channel through which repeated flows of reader energy produce new "narratives," each perhaps varying slightly but still identifiable as an instantiation of a specific narrative system. Narrative potential for continued activity is much greater than a closed system would allow.

The description above implies a narrative system that is essentially a textual artifact influenced by other, outside systems, such as readers and critics.[6] However, this description is deliberately simplistic, designed to illustrate the distinction between open and closed systems rather than to serve as a model for actual systemic functioning. To continue with such a limited figuration of the narrative system would be as reductive as to describe the human system as one which simply processes calories in an attempt to instantiate itself as a living being. Obviously, both are more complex. Humans are supersystems, autonomous networks of cooperative systems; similarly, narratives depend upon the interaction of systems that work together in the realization of a complex cultural construction. Like a human being, a narrative is so much a multisystemic product of ongoing processes involving complicated internal and external relations that it is (at least metaphorically) an autonomous infodynamic organism.[7]

The narrative supersystem, rather than being constituted by a text, is constituted by a network of relations between components that *include* a text; in order to produce the conceptual construct "narrative," processes involving a number of systems are required: an author system, a reader system, a critical system, and a textual system comprised of narratological and artifactual subsystems. Each of these systems is itself complex, having a structuro-functional[8] configuration similar to that of the supersystem, that is, one dependent upon a particular set of relations and components. These systems interact horizontally with other systems and vertically with the supersystem and with their own subsystems; in addition, each system may participate nodally in other supersystems.[9]

To clarify this notion of the narrative supersystem, let us take, for example, the Gatsby guest list. That particular list is actually a hyposystem in the *Gatsby* narrative system: it is a component of the narratological subsystem (the entire narrative strategy of *The Great Gatsby),* which is a component of the textual system (the construct resulting from the interaction of the narrative strategy and the physical artifact containing the text of *The Great Gatsby),* which is a component of the narrative supersystem (the *Gatsby* which exists as a cultural construct, along with all its actual and potential configurations of author constructions, reader constructions, textual representations, and critical expectations and interpretations).

In addition, however, the Gatsby guest list is a node which can participate in other systems outside the *Gatsby* supersystem. For instance, in the anecdote recounted earlier, the memorized guest list participates in a system that lies outside the boundaries of its home supersystem; its operative focus in this system is not a narratological one, but an epistemological and (later) a social one. Some of its activities have no effect on *Gatsby:* when the list serves as an information channel at the cocktail party, the message passed through the list does not affect the overall construction of *Gatsby*. On the other hand, its forays into the outside world have in fact attracted critical attention, if only the focused attention of this study; this attention may require some internal reconfiguration of the relation between the critical system and the textual system containing the list. Thus, the list is also a node which can serve as an intrasystemic interchange, a place where both the injection of critical energy into the narratological subsystem and subsequent restructuration of both the critical and the textual systems might occur.

Outside the *Gatsby* supersystem we find other narrative supersystems which may have systemic nodes that convey information to or from *Gatsby* (as a systemic energy source) but do not thereby *enter* the supersystem itself. For example, Gilbert Sorrentino's *Mulligan Stew* (1979) recycles Daisy Buchanan as a character and thus opens an interactive node between the two systems. The informative potential of this node insists upon a minute but pervasive reconfiguration of *Gatsby:* all systems are potentially altered by this interaction with *Mulligan Stew*. Similarly, the use of a *Gatsby* character has informative potential for *Mulligan Stew:* all systems must allow for system configurations that are *Gatsby* competent. Although neither system is absorbed by the other, this one interactive node holds a position in virtually every system in each narrative supersystem; in effect, each supersystem has caused a momentary perturbation in the other, and each has accommodated and controlled the chaotic potential of that perturbation.[10]

Simple hierarchical information systems may be graphically illustrated by means of a tree diagram. In this sort of representation, information transfer points, or nodes, are arranged in levels branching down from the root; nodes on the same level are roughly equivalent in importance, and a lateral sequence may even be assigned indicating a nonsimultaneous triggering of nodes on one level. Each node is joined to only one other node at any higher level though it may itself be the parent node for several lower nodes (Resnikoff 1989, 112). Narrative supersystems are themselves hierarchical, but this sort of representation cannot take into account supersystemic interaction at multiple nodes or the multiple roles played by any individual node in systems outside the supersystem hierarchy. Because systems are adaptable over time, any verbal description of a narrative supersystem is necessarily synchronic, and graphic representation is impossible without a multispatial medium that can also be configured for the temporal dimension.[11]

Since systemic formal structure is a function of internal configuration, and since that configuration may be adjusted to meet environmental demands, the external form of a system is relatively plastic.[12] Identity is preserved as long as the relations between components are constant—just as a human system remains identifiably itself under radically different formal conditions. Reconfiguration is limited only by what Varela calls the system's *cognitive domain,* which is the "domain of interaction that an autonomous system can enter through structural plasticity without loss of closure" (quoted in Paulson 1988, 162). As long as they do not transgress the borders of the cognitive domain, external structural boundaries may adapt to changing conditions without endangering the overall integrity of the system. The creation of an interactive node between *The Great Gatsby* and *Mulligan Stew* does not prevent *Gatsby* from achieving any of its narrative goals; indeed, that open node provides energy for intrasystemic restructuration, particularly in the critical system.

Some systems have no autonomy whatsoever. These tend to be simple message or energy transmission mechanisms, which are structurally implastic and have predetermined internal relations. Like an electric alarm clock, such a system performs externally designated functions until its structures decay or its power source is depleted or disconnected. In the face of environmental challenge, this system simply goes on unchanged or, if the challenge is a serious one, breaks down completely. The addition of feedback or monitoring processes to such a system permits it to refine and control its performance but still does not allow any structural or functional flexibility; it has no capacity for innovation or growth and hence a very limited capability for constructive response to chaos.

Complex monitoring processes move a system in the direction of autonomy and can be found in both artificial and natural systems, which Laszlo defines as those which do not owe their "existence to conscious human planning and execution" (1972, 23).[13] Natural systems are inherently autonomous. However, the autonomy of an artificial system is a function of its construction rather than a self-definition proceeding from the effective integration of systemic processes; the monitoring and regulation operations, for instance, are programmed into the system and do not arise naturally as responses to environmental or intrasystemic demands. Nor can an artificial system be *aware* of its monitoring processes except in the sense that a breakdown in processing may be signaled to some other control mechanism.

Narratives—as strategies and artifacts—are obviously artificial.[14] Narrative supersystems, however, gain definition and purpose from the processes that bind them together. While such systems might not be classifiable as "natural," they do exist at the margins of natural autonomy in a fuzzy logical zone where the conceptual construction of a complex network of relations, and the interaction of the structures inhabiting that network, can create an entity that is systemically coherent and functionally purposive.

Systemic complexity is closely related to autonomy. A system may be orderly and functional but have little information upon which to base restructuration decisions; an ordered structure may be "characterized by a high degree of redundancy and thus a low level of information," while a complex structure may have a "low level of redundancy and a high degree of information" (Paulson 1988, 72). Although a system requires

sufficient redundancy measures to ensure successful completion of processes, an autonomous system must not be so heavily
redundant that its decision-making capacity is impaired. Highly
complex monitoring and feedback structures allow a system to
balance these two needs; in complex structures, completion of
processes may result from a number of systemic operations that
are regulated by a multiplicity of monitor functions. At the high
end of complexity, extremely sophisticated monitoring mechanisms move complex autonomous systems toward the condition of subjectivity, from simple purposive behavior toward the
capacity for innovation.

A conceptual framework that permits autonomy in systems
involves a reinterpretation of systemic environment. To a mech-
anized system, the environment is simply a source of inputs
which generate relatively predictable outputs; to an autonomous
system, the environment is a source of demands for change,
a source of perturbations that require systemic compensations.
In a

> control-based formulation, interactions from the
> environment are instructive, constitute part of the
> definition of the system's organization, and de-
> termine the course of transformation. In [an]
> autonomy interpretation, the environment is seen
> as a source of perturbations independent of the
> definition of the system's organization, and
> hence intrinsically noninstructive; they can trig-
> ger, but not determine, the course of transforma-
> tion. (Varela, quoted in Paulson 1988, 122–23)[15]

My representation of the interactive node between *Mulligan
Stew* and *The Great Gatsby* assumes an interpretive framework
in which narrative supersystems act autonomously. In this
frame, Sorrentino's appropriation of "Daisy Buchanan" is not
an input requiring particular sorts of outputs in the *Gatsby*
supersystem; it is an environmental trigger for systemic decision making (and for potential reconfiguration, which may have

a number of intrasystemic or output effects). In other words, the figuration of *Gatsby* as an autonomous system implies response alternatives. And these response alternatives are made possible by (1) systemic plasticity and (2) complex monitoring processes.

Consider the task of input regulation: in a narrative supersystem several systems take part in this process, some as enablers, some as inhibitors. The author system, for instance, is the component that limits opportunistic invasions of the textual system by contracting with a publisher for printed versions of the text. Certainly, marginal notes can be added to any one artifact, but such additions have a very limited disruptive effect; they are not distributed across output copies, and they can be easily differentiated from print-version text by any reader. The reader system, on the other hand, has many nodal positions that facilitate extrasystemic input in the form of intertextual influences, codified expectations, and physical interruptions of the reading process. All these demand responses on the part of the overall system.

The task of functional evaluation is shared by the reader system, the author system, and the critical system; all are in a position to monitor the successful transmission of the supersystemic message, which in the case of *The Great Gatsby* would be: *"The Great Gatsby."* At this level, the message is of course the continued instantiation of the narrative; therefore, monitoring requires the surveillance and measurement of the status of all subsystems. Feedback occurs when monitoring indicates the need for adjustment: should the *The Great Gatsby* become so closely associated with *Mulligan Stew* that its separate existence as a supersystem is threatened, the critical system might institute differentiation processes; should *Gatsby* go out of print, the reader system or the critical system might begin archival action or initiate further publication to make sure the subsystem node occupied by textual artifacts is secure.

Nodal flexibility enables the narrative supersystem to fill positional demands quickly; many nodes have a stock of alternative positions that can be called upon as responses. The author system, for instance, can position itself as a social, legal, or critical construct rather than as a human being, as changes in the supersystemic environment may require. The narratological subsystem can be construed as a number of different strategies, all equally legitimate in the context of the overall message (instantiation of *The Great Gatsby*). And the reader system can be figured as any number of actual persons, or as a critical construct, or as a strategic space necessitated by narrative processes. In every case the supersystem maintains its component relations while adjusting itself to environmental perturbations and even incorporates extrasystemic information as energy or as material for restructuration.

One hesitates at the boundary between such an autonomous, even autopoietic,[16] system and one which exhibits consciousness. An autonomous system necessarily has what Laszlo calls subjectivity, that

> ability of a system to register internal and external forces affecting its existence in the form of sensations [which is] universal in nature's realms of organized complexity. (1972, 91)

However, for Laszlo, consciousness necessitates an *awareness* of subjectivity. Varela makes a similar distinction when he defines cognition as "adequate and self-consistent behavior in the face of perturbations and not as the establishment of representations of a reality outside the knowing system" (quoted in Paulson 1988, 162). Systemic consciousness can be identified only through its products: representations of self and environment that are separate from (but proceeding from) monitoring processes. By this definition, the narrative supersystem, though complex and powerful, is not a conscious entity; it creates *itself* through its processes but does not create *representations* of itself.[17]

An open system seeks a steady state, a balance between incoming information and outgoing entropy; the maintenance of such a state keeps it far from thermodynamic equilibrium, the condition of maximum predictability or heat dispersion that results from entropic processes.[18] An autonomous system, however, seeks chaos management; when faced with an influx of chaos (noise or perturbation), the autonomous system processes it as information, extending its own structural boundaries around the space of disorder or creating new structures into which the chaos can be absorbed. This management technique ensures the survival of the system as it renovates the structure of the system, and it increases the overall orderliness of the universe as more and more chaos material is transformed into order.[19]

Major systemic reconfiguration is a relatively common occurrence in the universe. Ilya Prigogine and Isabelle Stengers note that

> new types of structures may originate spontaneously. In far-from-equilibrium conditions we may have transformation from disorder, from thermal chaos, into order. New dynamic states of matter may originate, states that reflect the interaction of a given system with its surroundings. (1984, 12)

In other words, a system which is far from equilibrium (but which may have reached a steady state) may react to fluctuations with amplification and restructuration rather than a return to stasis; chaos management, and a new order, will be the result. In this systemic framework, turbulence carries a message and that message is "structural (or relational) change."

Alternatively, chaos management may require interpretive activity up or down the systemic hierarchy;[20] Prigogine and Stengers indicate that systemic monitors can assume that turbulence, though apparently an intrusion of noise or disorder into the system, is in fact highly organized at scales either above or below the norm of observation or description used for definition of the system (1984, 141). In order properly to interpret or process the turbulence, then, the monitor must access other levels or find an interpretive code that translates extralevel noise into information. Here, the initiation of pattern recognition functions and conceptual mapping operations may enable monitors to tranform "noise" into usable information.[21]

Since all systems produce noise during the course of operation and pass that noise on during nodal interaction, noise is generated and dispersed throughout the supersystem. In all horizontal and vertical systemic activities, then, one relation is constant: each system must be the observer and reader of every other system. Without intrasystemic chaos management, this multilevel production of noise would overwhelm the system; to ensure systemic health, each level must engage in the conversion of extralevel noise into information (Paulson 1988, 48). Indeed, it may be that with sufficiently sophisticated or extensive translation capacity, all noise will reveal itself as intrasystemic. Paulson suggests, in a discussion of Jurij Lotman's *The Structure of the Artistic Text* (1977), that in complex artistic systems there is no extrasystemic information, only polysystemic information that must finally (on one level or another, with one interpretive code or another) be assigned a role within the structure (1988, 86). In other words, there is no noise, only uninterpreted or misinterpreted information. Or, everything is connected.

Surprise Roast

There exists in the human mind an almost irresistible urge toward order, a tremendously powerful compulsion to determine and decipher patterns and structures. Indeed, the brain has sophisticated information-processing techniques that specifically operate to bring order out of the sensory chaos that threatens the orientation and function of the human system. These operations extend far outside the boundaries of the body, interacting with other, similarly organized systems and creating informational supersystems—social and cultural networks that incorporate humans as nodes in complicated articulate structures.[1] The essential relationality of all information and all systems makes sense in a global, ecological context; however, on the human scale, such totalization is a paranoid's nightmare come true, a world where everything is finally connected.[2]

A paranoid depends upon theories of global systematization even as he fears their confirmation; he needs and wants to be the node through which all information must flow, but he knows that such a position leaves him vulnerable to those who would locate, use, or destroy him. Consequently, his lunatic positioning at the center of an enclosing and encroaching structure is problematical; it is a position of both desire and danger. Inhabitation of that space requires regular and delicate manipulation of information so that the delusional structure can be maintained without crushing the paranoid under the weight of its ordering devices.

The line between a delusional structure and a coherent one is very fine. One always suspects, for instance, that Thomas Pynchon's characters are hovering on the edge of insanity, that events in the world cannot be as coherent as their various versions of global conspiracy would suggest. But conspiracy theories are as difficult to disprove as they are to prove. Proof suggests an ability to represent the entire system accurately, and this is virtually impossible, since no constituent component contains sufficient processing power for such a task. On the other hand, it is reasonable to extrapolate, to draw conceptual maps based on patterns of systemic behavior. It is possible—and epistemologically valid—to make guesses about the overall structure based upon the limited evidence at hand; and for Pynchon characters, the evidence suggests a frightening and dehumanizing coherence in the world.

Engaged in attempts to recognize and interpret the systemic structuring processes around them, processes which seem to threaten their agency and even their continued existence as either extrasystemic or intrasystemic objects, Pynchon characters inhabit the difficult position of the paranoid, fearing and desiring confirmation of their interpretive operations. In *Gravity's Rainbow* (1973), for example, the problem of identification and orientation is an overriding one; characters work desperately throughout the novel to recognize or establish their positions in relation to the System, and they manipulate information about these positions to maintain a (perhaps delusional) structure that grants them authority and autonomy.

Roger Mexico's triumph over the Krupp cartel is engineered precisely by the manipulation of information and structure. The battle takes place at a dinner party scheduled toward the end of the novel, at a time when the Zone is finally reintegrating itself and when many characters are being forced to declare their post-War affiliations. Mexico clearly wants to align himself with anti-Systemic forces. Wishing to inhabit a position outside the System, he hopes to construct that location out of oppositional relations. He thus refuses to allow the boundary between peace and war to serve as a limit around his love for Jessica Swann and attempts to locate and recuperate Slothrop (who has now passed outside the interest and surveillance of the Firm). Further, Mexico claims for himself a life of resistance to the efforts of Pointsman when he urinates on the "poker-faced men" who confer in Clive Mossmoon's office (636). He considers himself an outlaw; his goals are entirely anti-Systemic.[3]

Seaman Bodine, Roger's dinner date, also maintains oppositional relations with the System. As a smuggler, drug dealer, and deserter, his role is clearly anti-Systemic; all of these involve boundary transgressions that work to weaken the definition of the System itself, and all create perturbations that force reactions inside the System Bodine opposes. Further, as a clown and a grotesque figure of the American entrepreneur, he participates in a subversion of the system through ridicule, questioning the self-concept of the system and therefore the value or success of its functioning. Order is, after all, terribly serious. The analytic, classificatory impulse that creates more and more ludicrous and intricate rational structures is one that cannot laugh at its own desperate attempts to suppress or absorb chaos wherever it may be found. Laughter suggests a breakdown of order, some anomaly, some intrusion of the irrational; thus, to the System, the sound of laughter is the voice of the enemy, of the outsider who cannot be brought into the ordering system and whose laughter therefore signals a failure of totalization.[4]

The invitation to dinner comes from Jessica's lover, Jeremy, who is in the Zone as a member of Operation Backfire, a British attempt to locate and assemble abandoned A4 rockets; this alone would be reason for Mexico, the rejected lover, to feel uneasy about the social situation. In addition, however, the party is to take place at the home of an ex-member of

management at the Krupp works, a site Roger immediately recognizes as a center of Systemic influence. Anticipating reprisals
from Them because of the "Urinating Incident," he invites
Bodine along for protection, even though Bodine faces a death
sentence for desertion should *he* fall into Their hands.

Roger understands that the Krupp environment signifies
both concentrated power and the seduction of membership;
in accepting the invitation to dinner, he has to a small degree
acknowledged (and even activated or empowered) the attrac-
tion of that world.[5] Further, he realizes that the dinner constitutes a decision point, a personal historical crux.[6] Here he must
either confirm his inclination toward sedition, and risk the
punishment that will surely be imposed, or he must allow himself to be used to legitimize the System. Ironically, They have
designed a punishment that will suppress Roger's resistance
while it simultaneously incorporates him into the System; the
listing of "surprise roast" on the menu card, like the large bar-
becue pit at the far end of the table, is an announcement of Their
intentions. Reception and acknowledgment of this message
requires a response: Mexico, the object of the threat, must
either submit or resist. Submission or, alternatively, a fight to
the death, would presumably end with Roger turning on the spit,
and such a death would feed the System both literally and metaphorically. If he is not to reinforce the control of the System,
then he must escape the end he is programmed for: he must
become a nonparticipant at the feast, refusing to serve either as
dinner or diner.

Since he has entered the space of Systemic control, simple
refusal is problematical; he and Bodine must find a way to
remove themselves from the center of this network of power.
One way to do this, of course, is by overpowering or overload-
ing the system; a flow of energy down the preestablished
lanes of exit and entry would clear the way for an escape.[7]
Another way to leave the center of systemic attention is to re-
align the connections and relationships that create that center
and thus to change the way that particular information node
is ordered.

In order to do this, Mexico and Bodine must be able to recognize and evaluate the informative potential of the structure which has enclosed them. The structure of the dinner party and their position within it limits their movements and, in fact, negates their anti-Systemic stance by subsuming their opposition and defusing it. To move outside this systemic node, they must reactivate and reestablish that oppositional relation. This is something Mexico and Bodine are quite prepared to do, and if they are successful, they regain their freedom and their autonomy as an anti-System at once.

Opposition implies difference; in order to exit the System, Mexico and Bodine must find and reinforce the differences between themselves and the System. This project requires information about the very systemic node that has enclosed them. That information is deeply encoded at another level, in fact, within the menu that has alerted them to danger. Because the two rebels are functioning on two levels in the scene, they are able to carry out an act of interpretation that would otherwise be impossible; as components in the dinner-party system, they are metasystemic operators in relation to the menu system of which they are intrasystemic components. Their metasystemic reading and interpretation of the menu reveals the pattern break which not only carries information, but eventually offers a way out.

Since Mexico and Bodine, as potential "surprise roasts," are constituents of the very menu they must decode, they are doubly trapped: inside the house, as dinner guests, and inside the menu, as entrees. Logic tells them that escape from the menu implies an escape from the dinner party, since the functioning of the dinner party depends upon the functioning of the menu. Their first strategy must thus be either to oppose themselves to the other items on the menu (as, for instance, non-edible items) or to oppose themselves to the menu as operators upon rather than constituents of the menu.

They begin this move not by objecting to the cannibalistic excesses the current menu suggests but by exposing and exploiting a *gap* in the menu, an opening created by the very operation that encodes human flesh as an appropriate source of nourishment. A menu is, after all, structured by the relationality of the items within it; the foodstuffs it announces and inscribes are temporally, spatially, and categorically related. Further, the menu is a linguistically codified form of a meal pattern that conforms to a socially codified form of communal activity. This insistence upon codification and pattern means that a break in the pattern, or a violation of the code, carries information in a way that this rather predictable (and socially redundant) structure would not otherwise do. The irruption of human flesh into a conventional dinner-party menu not only has informative value, it fractures the cohesion of the structure itself, opening a gap through which systemic energy may flow in both directions. Mexico and Bodine recognize that break in the pattern as an opportunity for disruption and deconstruction, and they are quick to exploit it. Under the inspiration of Brigadier Pudding's spiritual guidance, their commentary becomes a "repulsive stratagem" of "culinary pranksterism" (715) that subverts and reinscribes the menu offered by the Krupp cartel; by gaining control of the construction process, they finally place themselves outside the menu and in a position of opposition and power.

The deconstruction and reinscription of the menu (itself a list structure) is enacted by a list dialogue, one which highlights the dishes that ultimately form the menu while it maintains connection (and parity) between the two rebels. The sole verbal interruption on the part of those who object to this disgusting reconstruction of their meal is a timid "I say"; ironically, the dissenter says nothing else at all and neither does anyone else. Instead, the erstwhile diners gag, vomit, rattle silverware, laugh nervously, and whisper to each other. But these sounds are the sign of loss of power, a failure to respond verbally to a verbal attack.

Initially only Bodine and Mexico participate in this act of de(re)construction, as they point out that the menu *ought* to offer

> snot soup, pus pudding, scum souffle, menstrual
> marmalade, smegma stew, clot casserole, after-
> birth appetizers, scab sandwiches, and booger
> biscuits spread with mucus mayonnaise and
> topped with slime sausage. (collated from 715)

However, as the list grows and as members of the System become nauseated and even begin to leave the table, other characters are drawn into the effort. First, newswoman "Commando" Connie understands and announces the process of selection ("Oh *I* see . . . it has to be al*lit*erative"[8]) and then offers her own additions to the list, "discharge dumplings and vomit vichyssoise." Soon after, the background music quartet joins in: the kazoo players offer "wart waffles" and "puke pancakes" while the cellist suggests "pinworm preserves." Finally, as Bodine and Mexico soft-shoe their way out the door, their disgusting little ditty about "Toe-jam tarts 'n' Diarrhea Dee-lite" accompanied by the full quartet, a black butler adds one last dish to the menu ("pimple pie with filth frosting, gentlemen") before he opens the "last door to the outside, and escape" (717).

The insertion of this list dialogue into the gap created by "Surprise Roast" stretches the existing menu structure as competitive menu items force the frame of the original menu to the margins. These new items fill and swell the center, making the gap the locus of anti-Systemic presence and instantiating a different set of relations between menu components; names of dishes must now be alliterative and substantively linked to the human body. Categorically denying inclusion even to "Surprise Roast," this tactic completely effaces the original menu. Like an invading virus, the new items overwhelm the host after using the information structure of the host as their point of entry. Essentially, Mexico and Bodine appropriate the space initially reserved for their own bodies and redefine that space as one which may be filled by any number of cannibal dishes; further, by moving up the logical scale from "member of the set" to "definer of the set" they exit the menu and place themselves outside that dangerous structure.[9]

Any meal depends upon anatomization for its structure; its temporal structure fragments and then reassembles blocks of time, and its culinary structure fragments the eating process into courses and/or dishes that are either temporally separated or spatially separated from one another. Indeed, this fragmentation is itself a cue or message about meal-ness; fragmentation has informative value for meal recognition. Further, foodstuffs are themselves subject to fragmentation during preparation or consumption. Death and dismemberment are appropriate in the realm of the culinary; it is the whole and living body that does violence to our notions of the edible.

The anti-menu Mexico and Bodine construct depends upon anatomization and fragmentation of the human body for its substance and for its subversive power. Every anatomization of the body is, according to Bakhtin, potentially culinary, since anatomization dismembers human corpses as if preparing them for a meal (1984, 192). Here, the rebels' linguistic play clearly figures the body as a pantry of ingredients; in fragmented form, the body can fill all the spaces on a menu, providing almost limitless opportunities for culinary invention. The threat of cannibalism which immediately precedes (and instigates) the creation of the menu gives force to this anatomization: had Mexico been roasted and eaten, the consumption of just these sorts of juices and organs might have been involved.

The reinscription of the menu exploits the opposition between improper food and proper food, between the unofficial body and the official one. Although proper diet has already been violated by the inclusion of "surprise roast" on the menu, the System's very ability to appropriate human flesh for culinary purposes foregrounds both the power of the System and its claim to property rights in the citizens under its dominance. Mexico and Bodine, by exaggerating the System's initial violation of food codes, point out the essential impropriety of the System's action in threatening them with consumption and incorporation. Questioning the System's right to power, they at the same time question official social structures and dietary codes.

Dietary codes and menu structures necessarily reflect and reinforce existing social structures. Mary Douglas, whose work has recently focused on the grammar of meals, writes that "if food is treated as a code, the messages it encodes will be found in the pattern of social relations being expressed. The message is about different degrees of hierarchy, inclusion and exclusion, boundaries and transactions across the boundaries" (1972, 61). She looks for the signification of any individual meal in its recognizable relationship to other meal events in the system; a common structure allows them to be analogized and permits gradation and classification, thus reinforcing the social structure of the culture (1972, 69). The anti-meal stands as antithesis to the regulated and cleanly meals demanded by the System and to the social codes that correlate food-stuffs with social position; as such, its relation is oppositional and revelatory. By constructing a menu from culturally forbidden items, Mexico and Bodine clarify and comment upon the classificatory processes of the culture.

Douglas further suggests that the purity of meal categories speaks to the general "sanctity of cognitive boundaries," that the integrity of physical forms helps protect the integrity of more abstract entities (1972, 76). The signification of Mexico and Bodine's anti-menu thus rests partly in its transgression of the boundaries of edibility and non-edibility; their redefinition of this boundary suggests that other boundaries might also be transgressed, that other categories might also be redefined.[10] This is revolutionary and represents a clear and present danger to the various kinds of boundaries and limitations defined and enforced by a hegemonic system.

Douglas points out that "whenever a people are aware of encroachment and danger, dietary rules controlling what goes into the body . . . serve as a vivid analogy of the corpus of their cultural categories at risk" (1972, 79). The System's preparations for a Mexico/Bodine roast suggest that human flesh may be acceptable under the rules set by the System; however, Systemic revulsion at the equally human dishes named by the rebels seems to define the battle as one over the power to define: only categories defined *by* the System can make the human body acceptable as meat. Any redefinition of the body, any restructuring of meal categories, questions the legitimacy of existing definitions and structures and threatens the power of the System.

We see opposed in this scene two versions of the body politic, the rigidly defined body against the fluid and amorphous body, the integrated body against the decomposed body or contingent body. A small revolution of one against the other takes place during the creation of the anti-menu. The rebels already stand at the margins of society; the woman, the musicians, the black man, the drug-dealing deserter, and a renegade statistician—these have little access to legitimate power within or sanctioned information about the System. As members, their activities are severely circumscribed by systemic processes and codified relations; as opponents on the margins, however, they may have the necessary autonomy for resistance to the totalization a globalized system implies. Of course, a system by definition has no truly marginal positions (only an inside and an outside), but the flexibility and permeability of structures permits a sort of border zone: in this space, changing relations keep the architecture of the network in question, and this is the location from which resistance to rigidification and domination may come.

The rebels openly reject the meal structure imposed upon them by the System and create an alternative vision of nutriment employing a grotesque anatomization of the body. This act of defiance unites them, establishing a contingent anti-System that is at least temporarily *outside* the system; at this point, they step over the margin, becoming components in a new, autonomous, and self-organized system that is clearly and coherently opposed to the one they have exited. Like Bakhtin's marketplace language, which unites the populace by opposing obscenity and impropriety to the conventionality of official speech, their repulsive repartee bonds them together by creating a "special collectivity, a group of people initiated in familiar intercourse" (1984, 188). As initiates, they are marked both by their facility in the jargon and by their ability to take delight in the obscene and the repellent.[11] Those not initiated to the world of the grotesque—the members of the System—are forced to flee the scene; and by their flight, they permit Mexico and Bodine to escape and at the same time acknowledge the power of language to resist and subvert the power of the System.[12]

David Seed sees the dinner-party scene in *Gravity's Rainbow* as having merely local disruptive effect; like the custard pie battle, he suggests, it offers comic relief from the "general complexities of the novel" as it "[temporarily demonstrates] an anarchistic exhilaration at breaking down the control of bureaucratic forces" (1988, 199). On the contrary, I see the scene as a model for the type of resistance to system Pynchon seems to advocate, a resistance that combines the efforts of the oppressed into an oppositional structure that is as effective as it is contingent.

In the end, of course, the dinner guests will stop vomiting; the members of the System will regroup and reestablish its control. Most of those involved in the creation of the anti-menu will eventually return to work for the System; indeed, "Commando" Connie, as the only diner to join the insurrection, can expect to "catch hell tomorrow" for her betrayal of social order. However, the marginal, anti-Systemic group does at least for the moment succeed in cohering, communicating, and working together to defuse the threat of death and/or co-optation.[13] In his epigraph to this section, Pynchon calls this sort of momentary collective the "dearest nation of all" (706).

The Mexico/Bodine collective is absolutely occasional, created in response to situational demands, enabled by the exploitation of existing structures and disassembled once its purpose is served. This is very different from the antisystem Pirate Prentice recommends. Prentice advocates a thoroughly coherent (if delusional) We-system engendered by "creative paranoia"

(638), a system which, ironically, might eventually rival the System itself if it attained any continuity as a social or political entity. The anti-menu Counterforce, however, is made possible only by a momentary coalescence of rebellious energies; its members refuse to submit to encapsulation, they escape through the interstices of the system and subvert totalization by engaging in the tactics of the margin. The success of Mexico and Bodine's "ad hoc adventure" suggests that it is necessary for a genuine antisystem to be fluid, to be fragmentary in its construction and limited in time and scope.

One conceptually (though perhaps not actually) global We-system that does have efficacy and continuity is the symbolic system of the banana, which is loosely constructed out of a series of ambiguous references following a relatively coherent statement of this antisystem's position. From a clearly oppositional space in Pirate Prentice's rooftop garden, where Prentice is on the roof picking bananas for breakfast when the "incoming mail" of the V2 rocket captures his attention (5–6), the system extends itself in brief, comic, and erratic manifestations throughout the novel: in an absent banana cream pie in Katje's bedroom (197), in the hands of performing chimpanzees on Frau Gnahb's boat (496), in Carmen Miranda hats worn by dwarves at the infinity point (664), and in Hogan Slothrop's Chiquita Banana masturbation fantasies (678). In each appearance, the banana (as representative of antisystem) declares its opposition to and persistence in spite of the competing global network that is represented by the missile.[14]

The banana is an anti-phallus, a grotesque erection clearly opposed to the patriarchal and martial missile phallus Prentice sees as he harvests his crop.[15] As a sign of alternative figuration and regenerative potentiality, the banana phallus defies phallogocentric repression and limitation as it simultaneously refutes the death message contained in the missile. The banana, an edible phallus, a rocket shape laden with sweet white meat, brings life instead of death; its heat is that of usable calories, its structure the genetic and molecular code that ensures an essential structural immortality.

When it comes down from the garden, the banana moves into a transformational matrix that opposes the sterile deformations of war, to a place where energies unite to ensure safety and satiation. Prentice's kitchen, and the groaning board of his Banana Breakfasts, together regularize an enclave of peace that is separate from the wartime regimen of death and dearth; within that space, encapsulated war images face consumption and erasure.[16] At breakfast, the bananas suggest a peacetime economy that fosters imagination and play as it affords sufficient time for culinary artistry; further, they speak of a cessation of hunger and need in a time when national resources are severely depleted and when what remains is carefully rationed and restricted. Thus, the banana concoctions are conceptual markers for a position that is temporally and economically outside the war zone. When breakfast is interrupted by the telephone and Prentice is recalled to the war, it becomes clear just how far away this scene is from the war: "a stretch of morning between [the breakfasters] and himself. A hundred miles of it, so suddenly" (11).

In effect, the Prentice household is outside the System; although it has communicational nodes that permit it to interact with and respond to systemic agents, it is a self-defined entity with completely different practices and purposes than those authorized by the System. Further, the breakfasts not only separate the house from the war, they offer protection via a mystical association of the inhabitants with the life-enhancing properties of the banana; offering spiritual as well as physical nourishment to the war-weary housemates, the Banana Breakfasts cast "a spell, against falling objects" (10). In a peculiar communion ritual, the housemates invest in, and are informed by, the structure of the banana at the same time as they participate in and are the structural constituents of a limited, inevitably transient, anti-System collective.

As a systemic symbol, the banana formalizes the relationship of structure to contingency, and of contingency to continuity. Like any complex structure, the banana antisystem is
plastic; it does not lose its identity under structural reconfiguration as long as its functional goals can be achieved. The bananas enter the kitchen precisely in order to be transformed, but
their essential banana-ness is never lost even in the automatic
blender: the aroma of the bananas Prentice purees for breakfast
wafts out across London, and this persistence of the banana's
structure even beyond its fragmentation and pulverization is
offered as a model of benign "assertion-through-structure" (10).

The aroma of bananas is informative in the context of war;
it announces a difference, an opposition to the stench of death.
The dissemination of that notice of difference is enabled by the
persistence of the banana's molecular structure and by a chemical code that asserts that structure. In similar fashion, the Banana Breakfasts are themselves a notice of difference, an
information structure encoding and asserting a distinction from
ordinary and orderly behavior. These are not, after all, normal
meals. The housemates consume an almost endless variety
of dishes:

> banana omelets, banana sandwiches, banana
> casseroles, mashed bananas molded in the shape
> of a British lion rampant, blended with eggs into
> a batter for French toast, squeezed out a pastry
> nozzle across the quivering creamy reaches of a
> banana blancmange to spell out the words *C'est
> magnifique, mais ce n'est pas la guerre* [. . .] tall
> cruets of pale banana syrup to pour oozing over
> banana waffles, [. . .] banana mead . . . banana
> croissants and banana kreplach, and banana oat-
> meal and banana jam and banana bread, and
> bananas flamed in ancient brandy Pirate brought
> back last year from a cellar in the Pyrenees also
> containing a clandestine radio transmitter . . .
> (10).

In this process of consumption, the housemates declare and privilege a taste that most would consider aberrant. The breakfasts are a small but significant act of rebellion against systematized behavior.

Prentice's banana trees are planted in a rooftop "impasto" of "unbelievable black topsoil" made of decomposed pharmaceutical plants, pig manure, dead leaves, and the "odd unstomachable meal" left or vomited onto the roof (5). Rising out of a bizarre medium, these precious fruits[17] are then served to a vulgar collection of housemates, who wait "drooling" as Prentice places the huge bananas in the blender.[18] The banana dishes themselves strike one as almost "unstomachable" even in wartime; this daily consumption of extravagant concoctions is surely an exaggeration of taste, an act of bravado rather than of appetite. A performative statement, the ritual of the Banana Breakfast enacts difference even as it asserts a thematic separation of the Prentice household from the rhetoric of war; the participants thus constitute a gustatory resistance force against conformity and restriction, and against membership in the System. The cultivation of "minority tastes" in food and sex establishes a space for opposition (Stark 1980, 68–69), and the Banana Breakfast, like the Candy Drill[19] and the various sexual deviations adopted by war-zone inhabitants, bonds the partakers into a contingent anti-System similar to the one that forms later at the dinner party.

Like the anti-menu, the anti-taste has informative and differential value. A deliberate adoption of behaviors labeled perverse by the System questions the social code that presumes to type behavior; it forces the assumptions underlying that code out into the open, where its structure can be examined and perhaps exploited for the resistance. One thing that is concealed by prescriptions of taste (and taste-bound behavior) is that the Systemically sanctioned taste is actually only one taste among many; when challenged by the anti-taste, it loses its dominant position and falls back into the pool of taste alternatives.

The list of breakfast dishes assembles variant forms of bananas, mirroring the multiplicity of forms underlying all taste selections. The structure of this list depends upon notions of permutation, of ringing the changes on a single concept or moving a form through all its possible states. Its use in this context suggests that permutation is the repressed substructure of the cultural code. Similarly, a permutational substructure lies beneath the cultural construct we know as narrative, since the narrative selected for presentation arises out of and at the expense of all other possible narrative designs. Thus, the Banana Breakfast list celebrates formal diversity and represents the transformational and permutational possibilities inherent in both language and the physical world.[20] Indeed, the permutated list itself, though apparently categorically static, tests its own limits by pressing the conventional out toward the borders of the possible and the improbable, paradoxically interrogating the concept of rigidly defined categories.

Although the missile will dominate the novel and finally hang suspended over the novel's conclusion, the banana concoctions seem to prophesy the ultimate defeat, or at least the inevitable transformation, of phallic structures. The pureed banana mocks the missile phallus, slyly hinting that it too could be blenderized: the radical deconstruction of the banana in preparation for breakfast assumes both phalloid shapes into an ontology that insists upon the eventual destruction of all forms in the quest for regeneration. The eternal hesitation of the concluding missile suggests that the constructive (and symbolic) potential of its parent system is finally rigid and sterile, that a blenderized missile cannot regenerate or reassert itself by communicating its structure to viable system agents. The banana, on the other hand, is liberated from phalloid stagnation by its deconstruction, and as it spreads its "kind scent" over Chelsea, "Death is told . . . clearly to fuck off" (10).

The antisystem symbolized by the banana is a subtle and elusive one. Since it privileges contingency and indeterminacy, it rarely surfaces as a coherent conceptual structure which can be measured against the System symbolized by the missile. Instead, it presents itself as a pattern of behavior, or perhaps a pattern of oppositional statements, which must be recognized and decoded before it can be identified as an autonomous and active entity. The momentary congregation of anti-Systemic forces at the dinner party is simply one of its manifestations.

In global terms, the anti-System refuses the sort of totalization sought by the System; it favors chaos-management processes which lead to creative restructuration over those which suppress or filter out turbulence. Pattern, in the anti-System, is asserted rather than imposed; this suggests that structuration is bivalent, that order can be positive as well as negative. Motivation, or context, is everything.

One feels less inclined to paranoia when faced with such systematization, more willing to believe that systemic forces are facilitative rather than restrictive. However, we have circled round to the edge of insanity here. If the anti-System is not (as Pirate Prentice suggested) created out of paranoia, not finally an entirely delusional structure, it is at least possible that the anti-System is actually a constituent node of the overarching System. As such, it could still maintain an intrasystemic identity and some amount of autonomy in the performance of its tasks. However, its purpose would be defined by its relations to, and possibly be subordinated to, the overall purpose of the System, which is, of course, the instantiation and maintenance of itself *as* a system. If this were true, then the anti-System might be a sort of cybernetic device, designed to provide feedback to the system and to regulate its processes to minimize excessive performance. Alternatively, the anti-System might function as a chaos-management node, containing (and eventually processing) the influctuation of disorder that might otherwise disable the system. Under either dispensation, Pynchon's paranoid characters would receive the confirmation of global structuration they so deeply desire and fear: that they do indeed inhabit a world where all information structures, and all positions of agency, are always already inside the system.

chapter 5

Patterns within Patterns

Information is a difference which makes
a difference.

—Gregory Bateson
Steps to an Ecology of Mind

Just as a supersystem is made up of coherent
and cooperative systems, all connected by sets of discrete and
identifiable relations, so is a system made up of components that
have established and recognizable relations to each other. A
textual system, for instance, is constituted out of and by means
of the relations existing between its narratological component
and its artifactual one: its intrasystemic narratological nodes
anticipate and inform artifactual nodes, which represent and
likewise inform the narratological nodes. The textual system
simply cannot function as an entity without these mutually
constitutive interactions between its two components.

The relations existing between two components in a system
are partly representative of location and duration, of an inter-
section of spatial and temporal axes. A more significant element
in the relationship, however, is the information path that is represented there. The two components communicate, recursively,
and the information exchanged between them enables
and controls their processes. In other words, an artifactual
response to narratological strategy is dependent upon receipt

of information that can direct physical embodiment of narrative; narratological responses to anticipated or actual artifactual structuration affect strategic decision making about and/or potential interpretations of that narrative.[1]

The activities of a system are all directed toward establishing and maintaining form, whether that form be physical or conceptual, or some configuration of dynamic forces. In the process, the system employs sophisticated information-management techniques which ultimately depend upon and follow from the acknowledgment of and notification of structural difference. This notification of difference then serves as information for further processing and structuring behavior, both within the system and in the system's external interactions; systemic organization thus depends upon recursive operations which code, transfer, and translate significant data.

The selection and translation of data into a form that can be passed from narrator to reader (or from narrator to critical self) structures *The Great Gatsby,* duplicating the structuration dynamic in the relation between the narratological strategy and the textual artifact; it also constructs Nick Carraway as the narrator: Carraway's task is to choose data that, once coded, can inform a transmissible structure that somehow represents (or, carries the message of) Jay Gatsby. He cannot provide a replication of Gatsby; such a replication assumes almost infinite knowledge and indeed an unlimited transmission channel capable of containing and transferring *every* datum which is (or might possibly be) related to the Gatsby story. Nor would such a replication align itself with Carraway's role *as* narrator, which assumes a selective and evaluative function in its very definition. Thus, Carraway must filter the data to find those which are both significant and transferable; and he must process the data through selection and codification operations in order to prevent an overload condition that would otherwise permeate and disfigure his information structure.[2]

Uncontrolled raw data (whether generated by intrasystemic components or insinuated by extrasystemic agents) can overwhelm a system. Human systems, for instance, are so data absorptive that research into sensory processing indicates there is no limit to the amount of information they can perceive; there is, however, a limit to how much they can cognitively process: the capacity of the human data-transmission channel is very great; the capacity of receiver locations to convert raw data into usable concepts is actually quite small (Dretske 1981, 148). All systems face a similar problem; limited by structural constraints on processing capacity, they must find a way to engage information reception and transmission procedures without exhausting internal resources or impeding structuration functions with unprocessed data. In order to maintain itself, a system must filter out noninformative material, monitor the flow of data, and institute means by which it can make decisions based on minimal input; consequently, a system needs screening devices, traffic control measures, and identification operations.

In the course of these operations, a system performs functions similar to those enacted at supersystemic levels; the potentially threatening chaos of internal and external datic perturbations is tamed by filtration, channeled absorption, and restructuration until the (reduced and altered) data become systemic material. Selective omission or reorganization of data, as well as the hierarchization of information structures, are processes integral to the categorization implied by such systematization.[3] The human visual system uses these functions during texture discrimination and edge detection: a mass of information is filtered and limited to a *sufficient* amount for discrimination, and then pattern classification and recognition are based upon the new, filtered data base. Here, categorization prevents an overload on the system, since much less information is required for texture identification than for complete description of a surface (Resnikoff 1989, 265–66).

This beneficial simplification is aided by the universal prevalence and persistence of patterns, which convey information about their own internal relations and about the structures that can represent or contain those relations. One advantage of patterns is that a discernible relationship between members of an information set permits us to make guesses about the content of the whole set even when only some members are actually present (Bateson 1972, 413). Another is that a pattern implies a particular spatiotemporal or logical structure. The pattern is not the structure itself, but rather a repetitive behavior that we conceive as a statement of relation between things; recognition of the pattern then allows us to extrapolate a structure that is logically linked to the relation that has been deduced.[4]

Pattern recognition is highly efficient, since this process uses preexisting templates which have been coded during concept formation; these coded templates increase recognition speed because the pattern need not be complete for a cognitive association to occur. The visual processing system, for example, uses "boundary conditions" to generalize to the outline of an image; this operation is known as *pattern continuation*[5] and involves a deduction of overall pattern from the known boundaries and general laws applying to the overt parts.

The transfer of information via patterns and their accompanying structures is energy efficient as well. Here, pattern recognition functions as a redundancy measure which helps ensure the accurate transmission of a message. Information theorist Claude Shannon's formulations indicate that structural redundancy consumes less energy (or channel space) than repetition of messages (Paulson 1988, 60). Thus, an efficient reinforcement of the message "dialogue" occurs when pairs of quotation marks surround blocks of text creating an artifactual structure experientially associated with narratological units containing dialogue.[6]

However, a pattern performs a more important, differential function. The presence of a pattern suggests an organizing principle at work, a systematization of data that, in its relations and implied structures, is inherently informative. Patterns, then, help distinguish information from noise and the formed from the formless. From this perspective, pattern recognition is a critical operation in the complex evaluative and transformational process that turns raw data into the structural material of signification.

A specific pattern of relations suggests (or insists upon) a particular physical structure. Thus, though we actually encounter the square before a recognition of its relations is made (before we associate the shape before us with the template for "parallelograms with equal sides and equal angles" stored in our concept inventory), the square is structurally instantiated *by those relations* and cognitively instantiated only when those relations have been recognized. Until then, it is only a nameless shape.

That recognition, that association of relation and structure, is the key to information. Since pattern recognition enables a preliminary distinction between noise and information,[7] it facilitates the identification of difference that enables an assertion of significance. Hofstadter notes that the process of pattern recognition involves several steps: (1) a search for *sameness* and an addition of *difference*; (2) a description of form; (3) a comparison with other forms; (4) a restructuration of descriptions by adding information, discarding information, or using another scale of measurement or angle of observation; and (5) a repetition of the process until the *difference* becomes clear (1979, 649). When the difference has been identified, then the *name* of the difference can be transmitted. Ultimately, signification depends upon the separation of the nameless from the named and upon the subsequent transmission of the name (or the structure) to a location where the semantic content of the name (or the structure) can become part of another information economy.

The narratological component of *The Great Gatsby* is a function of internal operations that categorize data and transmit formal codes in a structural language. As noted earlier, *Gatsby*'s entire systemic structure suggests a realization of pattern recognition and formal transmission, and certainly its narrative strategy is initiated by Nick Carraway's attempts to collect, filter, and categorize information about Jay Gatsby. And that strategy is formalized by Carraway's subsequent codification of information into a transferable structure. Thus,

Carraway's narrative is informed by his information-processing endeavors, which are themselves informed by the patterns into which Gatsby data clusters resolve over time.[8] Indeed, a multiscalar recursive symmetry, encoding pattern recognition and translation procedures, operates between and across each systemic level so that the *Gatsby* supersystem is pattern dependent at any point of observation.

Carraway's problem is initially one of filtration, of how to separate the significant (or explanatory) from the insignificant. He logically moves to do this through categorization as he attempts to find *patterns* in the raw data pool constituted by the events of the summer of 1922. Trips in and out of the city coalesce, retrospectively, into one sort of pattern, a cause-and-effect relationship that he structures as narration because of the obviously sequential nature of such a relation. The parties at Gatsby's house, on the other hand, resolve themselves into a relation constituted by membership, and he structures that relation as a list because of its set-bound nature. Clearly, these structural units respond to the relations Carraway identifies in their constituent data; patterns exhibited in the data pool then ripple upward throughout the system via structural information and actualization operations. Structural alternations of, or thematic coordination between, sequential relations and membership relations recur at every level of the *Gatsby* supersystem. *Gatsby* is thus self-organizing and self-similar.[9]

In communication theory, the information value of any structure is a function of the relative unpredictability of its structural components and the translation (and/or processing) capacity of the receiver. For example, if the data in Carraway's narrative are entirely predictable, then they are redundant (or perhaps archival) rather than informative; in fact, since communication involves serial transmissions of data from a known (in narrative, linguistically possible) data pool, the relative improbability of any single transmission is the best measure of the transmission's informational content (Resnikoff 1989, 13).[10] A message without novelty, or without a registration of difference, is no message at all; it is simply a confirmation of what is already known.

Carraway's information-processing activities are thus constrained by the expectations of his potential receiver: for his overall narrative to be effective (informative) it must contain notification of difference. The registration of that difference may be associated with his method; he may assert a perception of different relations among the Gatsby data which justifies (and demands) new structuration processes for instantiation of those relations. Or the registration may be made in a difference of position; Carraway may claim a metasystemic location (or a variant scale of measurement) which permits (indeed, insists upon) new models of relationship, perhaps encoding interscalar connections invisible at other locations. Finally, the difference encoded in his narrative may simply be an acknowledgment of (or filtration of) *different* patterns (or clusters of data) than have hitherto been recorded.

The "difference" linked with information in communication theory has little connection to the "différance" Jacques Derrida promotes; in communication theory, difference registers a clear and unambiguous distinction from either preceding messages, predictable transmissions, or unspecific noise. However, a "deconstructivist" move toward the privileging of ambiguity is evident in some recent work on information transmission within complex systems. Henri Atlan notes that although a received message having "destructive ambiguity" (or corruption or noise) has less informative value than a clear message,[11] a received message having "autonomy-ambiguity" has *gained* informative value in the corruption process; in the latter case, an organizing system has converted "a loss of specificity in communication into a gain in overall complexity," a complexity which has inherent value because it contains informative *potential* (Paulson 1988, 74). Ambiguity can thus be absorbed into a self-organizing system as material for future structuration.

For conventional communication, the content of the message must not only register difference but have an appropriate (and viable) decodification context as well; the encoded data must decompose into signs which have relevance in the world of the receiver. And the transmission structure itself must be decipherable—if Carraway's receiver does not understand that a narrative implies causal and temporal sequence and that a list implies a selection process which links members to each other and to a categorical concept—then the structure is informatively empty.[12] Without competent decoding, data (no matter how orderly) are simply noise.

Nick Carraway's narratological structures are complex coding devices that convey messages about Gatsby while they comment upon Gatsby's relationship to the patterns Carraway has identified. The blocks of causal narrative suggest that Gatsby himself is a translation code which transforms the events of that summer into precursers and signs; in a symmetrical operation, Gatsby's personal significance is encoded in (and revealed by) the ordering structures that form around him. Similarly, the list suggests that Gatsby orders his Long Island universe, that he defines sets which would otherwise be unclassifiable, as it simultaneously implies that these Gatsby-defined sets encode semantic statements about Gatsby that can only be understood in terms of category and class.

Carraway's coded structures are information processors, vehicles for the transmission of forms from one system to another, a process that necessarily implies an expectation that the form will arrive at its destination intact (Young 1987, 61).[13] The instantiation of *Gatsby* is indeed the end product of a chain of such information processors, a series of isomorphic transportation structures that move a single statement ("Gatsby") from one place to another so that it can be deciphered and recoded before being transmitted again. The significance of the system rests entirely in this symmetrical and repetitive process, the formation and information of conceptually and structurally linked logical entities.

For a human system, meaning is a transform of information, the translation and restructuration of data into cognitive structures;[14] for non-conscious systems, however, transforms of information simply result in further configurative operations that track sets of relations as they appear or are made possible by the "news of difference" carried by precedent infostructures.[15] The system itself never represents its activities to itself as having (or attaining) significance; it measures its success in the maintenance of structure and process. New order is a systemic bonus, created out of chaos-management operations that find information in statements of difference. Indeed, Bateson insists that "no new order or pattern can be created without *information*" (1979, 45). This seems counterintuitive; our inclination is to say that existing data can easily be rearranged, recodified into an order that carries different signification. However, any such reorganization necessarily depends upon reinterpretation or even upon an invocation of randomization; either act is differential and thus informative.

Coding of difference results in particular sorts of structures, according to whether the difference is registered digitally or analogically. Digital forms involve a binary distinction between two oppositions or states: a lighted computer screen means the system is on; a dark one, off. A digital structure might encode a representation of Gatsby, for example, as a series of choices between opposing traits: honest/dishonest, simple/complex, tender/tough, and so forth. Analog representations, on the other hand, change as conditions change: the mercury in a thermometer changes position as the temperature increases or decreases. In a narratological context, a conventional narration of events may be closest to analogical representation. In this case, the narrative moves forward (spatially, temporally, and strategically) as events in the story move forward.

Analog representations are rich in data but require considerable structural space for the encoding of difference and high levels of processing energy for the analysis or decipherment of that difference.[16] Digital representations are efficient, but the conversion of information into a digital (classified or generalized) form necessitates a certain loss of information (Dretske 1981, 141). A digital representation of Gatsby, for instance, erases all the gradations *between* simplicity and complexity, or honesty and dishonesty. Whatever benefit might have been gained from an acknowledgment of intermediary (or ambiguous) states is lost.

In addition, the informational foundation of the semantic statement[17] being encoded is obscured by a digital structure. Digital encodings of information conceal nested information which would be visible in an analogical representation; thus, a structure naming Gatsby a bootlegger conceals associative information that a narrative about bootlegging would expose. A digital representation may even be deliberately deceptive, structured via a controlled learning situation so that "bootlegger" is incorrectly linked with a template for some other concept.[18]

Any digitalized label attached to Gatsby tends to conceal Carraway's filtration and hierarchization processes and to efface his role as narrator; further, it works to conceal the richness (and potential ambiguity) of the data pool which attracted Carraway in the first place. However, some digitalization is necessary, if only for the sake of economy. Otherwise, the project returns to an effort at replication, which would, after all, produce the perfect Gatsby analog.

Curiously, the ubiquitous guest list is both analogical and digital. As a list, it is essentially digital in conception and construction. Conceptually, it constitutes itself as a singularity, a differential category that has a unique and perceptible name. Structurally, it embodies a series of binary selections that, upon codification and hierarchization, result in an architecture of difference. The name of the list is "the names of those who came to Gatsby's house that summer" (61) and its name reveals its fundamentally binary nature: digital statements are here encoded about a single type of information, one relevant location, and a unique time frame.[19] Data referring to people who visited Gatsby at some other location in some other year and season are not to be included; those data are forever "outside" in terms of the inside/outside opposition which is the essence of a set.

On the other hand, the guest list is at least partially analogical; it attempts to represent a fullness, to indicate by its detail a comparably full set. By its length, the list suggests an extensive social acquaintance; by its various syntactical approaches, a diverse assemblage; by its colloquialism, a reference to class. Any of these statements might have been made digitally with greater textual economy and more precision. However, this encoding of analogy inside an essentially digital structure subverts the binary form of the list and empowers the ambiguous data that do find an entrance into the set.

The guest list violates its digital premises in several ways. First, the list includes a great deal more than is advertised: in addition to "names," it offers addresses, occupations, and occasional histories. Second, some of the names themselves are dubious; for instance, "the Chrysties" are exposed as "Hubert Auerbach and Mr. Chrystie's wife" (61), a prince (whose name Carraway has "forgotten") is addressed as a Duke (63), and Benny McClenahan's "girls" interchange with identical sets of McClenahan girls whose names may be "Jacqueline, . . . or else Consuela, or Gloria or Judy or June" (63). Finally, one of the guests appears at Gatsby's so often as to escape his categorization and enter a new category as "the boarder" (62).

The condition of ambiguity into which this digital structure enters is exacerbated when Carraway reveals that the list is not, after all, a complete record of party guests but merely a collation of recollected names. This suggests that at least some of the names may be included incorrectly (that the names may in fact apply to some other categorical context) and that a significant number of actual guests may have been left off Carraway's list.

Carraway's failure to encode his structures precisely or to find structures impervious to noise does not invalidate his transmission operations; all formal transactions are subject to deviation during encoding and transmission processes. As long as relations are generally stable, the transmission may be considered successful; minor corruption can be overcome through pattern recognition and reconstitution operations. In fact, although communication experts struggle to minimize deviation, narrative systems take advantage of noise and eagerly incorporate it when possible; narrative chaos finally enhances the system's viability.

Binary or digital forms of information are inevitably ambiguous, since the gap between the poles of an opposition leaves room for (perhaps even invites) chaotic intrusions. Analogical forms tend away from precision, since fewer evaluative or filtration processes mediate between the data and the information form; the receiver encounters relatively raw data which must then be hierarchized and categorized as the infostructure is decoded. This unmediated encounter permits chaos to enter into the system during decipherment when inappropriate contextualizations or misapprehensions of structure are likely. Further, analogical structures necessarily contain a great deal of noise when correlated with specific uses; they offer a great deal more information than required for simple decision making. Clearly, there is no perfect information structure and no way to ensure perfect transmission.

Complex systems thrive on imperfection, on environmental challenge and ambiguous data. Predictability and precision actually squelch the recuperative and reconstructive processes that enable complex systems to extend their operations; without internal or external chaos to manage, such systems become unregenerative, inert, and doomed to instantiation within replicable and predictable structures. In a perfect universe, information is totalized and controlled, and systems lose the power to reconfigure reality. With sufficient variation and difficulty in the data pool, however, systems flourish, inhabiting a region that fluctuates between order and chaos.

chapter 6

Two Hundred Whores

Pynchon's list of banana concoctions, in addition to initiating a discourse dependent upon phallic metaphors, leads us into the world of linguistic excess. His paranoiac systematization of the phallus is focused upon an excess of control; thus, as the reader eventually comes to understand that intersecting systems of knowledge mean not greater control *of* but indeed greater control *by* information, she begins, as Robert Hipkiss suggests, to realize that Pynchon is offering an antisystem to which access can only be gained through the fostering of surprise, the acceptance of indeterminacy, the refusal to reconcile opposing forces, and the utilization of transfer points from one system to another (1984, 30).

The antisystem is the world of excess and exhaustion; a plethora of alternatives ensures that opposing forces *cannot* be reconciled, as if the ground of the excluded middle suddenly became solid. Here, a capacity for negative capability is essential if the oppositions we depend on for rationality are not to collapse into an abyss of ambiguity. Here, the list's inherent deconstructibility is abruptly exposed, and this fissure in the structure of human order opens on an expanse of disruptive linguistic play.

The list, which initially seems the very embodiment of order, a *visible* system, has a natural tendency to tip toward a subversion of the systematic. This tendency lends itself to exploitation by the contemporary author who seeks to discover the limits of narrative. The spatial, temporal, and linguistic conventions of the list thus become metaphors of larger conventions— iconic forms within an exhausted, equally iconic form that, to John Barth at least, is ripe for replenishment.

An information structure like the list is laden with meaning, is overdetermined and bloated with cultural allusion. When it is also *visibly* excessive, a radical reinterpretation and reassessment of the information contained within it is *obviously* called for: the excessive list is as blatant as a billboard.

Under the pressure of reassessment, such a list ultimately reveals either the poverty of the system behind it or the impossibility of an accurate and complete naming of parts; when this impotence is recognized, the foundation beneath the structure (the belief system beneath the information system) is called into question. The possibility of a failure of order must then be recognized; if ordering devices are impotent in the face of reality, then we must posit a world where chaos and ambiguity can be only temporarily held at bay.

Inhabiting such a position might be dismaying for some; Barth, however, uses a reassessment of information structures to create a novel that questions the very nature of knowledge. *The Sot-Weed Factor* (1967) presses many sorts of information structures to their limits; the novel teems with verse, tales, lists, games, the exposition of philosophical and moral oppositions, and various forms of written documents (journals, poems, contracts, depositions, financial accounts, commissions). The novel itself is structured around the exhaustion of possibilities, and the exhaustive, excessive, *alternative* nature of history is foregrounded until that too can be seen as an ordering device with inherent limitations.

The Sot-Weed Factor is in many ways a Rabelaisian text; episodic, bawdy, and culturally detailed, the novel is both thematically and physically outsized—as are some of the lists it contains. Many of these lists mirror lists in the work of Rabelais: books, bum-wipes, curses, and foods self-consciously reflect precedents set in *Gargantua and Pantagruel*. Small lists present themselves at every turn, but the list of synonyms for "whore," the list of foods eaten at the Ahatchwhoop's banquet, and the list of twins are genuinely Gargantuan as well as Rabelaisian. These lists, monstrous in form, slip the bonds of orderly information processing, pushing our experience of the narrative toward an immersion in excess.

Such lists are *evidently* excessive, not just morally or thematically beyond the pale. A Gargantuan list takes up too much space on the page; its nature is physical as well as meaningful. Because it forces a shift in visual tracking and even in the pace of comprehension, this sort of list impedes the reading process; the drag of the list tends to pull the reader out of the text and into a recognition of textual strategy. It thus acts as a sort of ladder, an intersystemic transit point by means of which the reader is invited to climb in and out of the narrative. Attempts to ignore this invitation are fruitless: the very act of rejection requires a conscious decision and hence a participation in the interactive and optional nature of reading.

Further, the Gargantuan list panders to our taste for the monstrous. By transgressing the limits of sufficiency, it opens the realm of overabundance; it permits us to wallow in words, to fill our senses with the sound and shape of them. We may even feel that *frisson* of revulsion that comes with genuine excess, a revulsion that comes not from moral inhibition but from fear of being overloaded, engulfed, smothered, buried. Susan Stewart, in her study of the gigantic, points out that in Rabelais's

> colloquy between Pantagruel and Panurge on the "virtues of Triboulet" . . . there is a threat of an infinite series of juxtaposed adjectives, as if language could clone itself into perpetuity without the need of returning "to earth." (1984, 90)[1]

The threat Stewart identifies lies in the loss of narrator- or reader-centered control suggested by a self-generating list, and the presence of such a threat, ironically increases the pleasure to be derived from an immersion in excess.

This pleasure is similar to the pleasure-in-destruction described by Georges Bataille in *Visions of Excess*. In this collection of essays, and particularly in the chapter titled "The Use Value of D. A. F. de Sade," Bataille opposes the repressed, moralistic, and exploited man—the man seeking order in construction—to the orgiastic, excretory, ecstatic, and ultimately free man who seeks release and renewal in excessive activity that ends in disorder and destruction (1985, 99). An orgiastic frenzy of words leads quite naturally to disorder, to a disruption of order and ordering behavior; Bataille would suggest, then, that the excessive list releases the narrative from linearity and opens, through destruction, a window on freedom.

Like whores, these excessive lists make overt statements about objectified pleasure. Indeed, pleasure and wonder dominate our first reactions to them. Pynchon's banana phallus generates a list that amuses and intrigues; Barth's grotesque Maryland generates a list that leaves us awed by Barth's linguistic virtuosity. This monstrous list containing, in fact, *over* two hundred words for "whore" (half of them in French) runs over six pages in the hardcover edition and occurs about midway through a novel that is largely concerned with definitions of and distinctions between the poles of certain oppositions.[2] One quite central opposition is fostered by the protagonist, Ebenezer Cooke, who has vowed to remain a virgin and to be the poet of virginity as well as Poet Laureate of Maryland. This virginity is opposed by two sorts of carnal knowledge: penetration of and experience of the world (embodied in Cooke's tutor, Henry Burlingame III) and penetration of and experience of the flesh (embodied in Cooke's eventual wife, the whore Joan Toast).

Cooke's avowed virginity is not a state given to excess, and he thus has no list of his own to set against that of the whores. In fact the question arises, *are* there two hundred words for virgin? I bow to Barth's greater vocabulary, but I strongly suspect there are not. And if not, then a remarkable linguistic disparity is marked in the list that *does* find its way to the pages of *The Sot-Weed Factor*. Perhaps "virgin" is so precisely descriptive that it is sufficient; perhaps "whore" is too simple and spare for a state so rich in sensation and narrative possibility. In any case, Barth makes use of this disparity by foregrounding it, setting the single "virgin" against the seemingly endless "whores," and calling the reader's attention to the fact that since virgins are so rare as to be almost nonexistent, the word hardly ever requires a synonym.[3]

The apparent opposition that is expressed when Ebenezer stands alone as the single virgin amid a wealth of whores is collapsed within Ebenezer himself. Although Ebenezer lays claim to an increasingly technical sexual virginity, he is from the beginning of the novel open and available to all comers. Easily influenced, he constantly hands over his loyalty and imagination to others, demanding only a bit of flattery or a convincing tale as payment. Easily deceived, he can be used by anyone who has the necessary coin: a glib tongue or a flair for deception. Thus, while he is able to remain a "virgin," he is led to participate at least vicariously in political intrigue, high-stakes gambling, piracy, the perversion of law, the suborning of indentured servants, and rape. He loses all moral, emotional, and intellectual innocence long before he consummates his marriage with the whore Joan Toast.

The list of "whores" is generated by a name-calling match which actually begins when Ebenezer calls Susan Warren (Joan Toast in disguise) a "thankless strumpet" (440); she flees from him and he follows in order to apologize. An almost self-symmetrical narrative recursion, the action in the next few pages serves as a sort of plot summary of the novel up to this point: Ebenezer (slowed by sickness) is "unable to move with any haste or efficiency" and soon loses track of Susan; he wanders "through a number of empty rooms, uncertain of his objective"; he encounters three whores, who drive him away with their barrage of insults; and finally he is driven by illness and by his inability to discriminate among alternatives to contract a marriage with the very woman he derided as a "thankless strumpet."

Ebenezer's encounter with the three whores is a telling one. Characteristically, he mistakes their position in the household, addressing them as servants, for he is rarely able to recognize people for what they are. They correct him, and the match is begun, the English whore and the French battling for supremacy in the vocabulary of their profession. Some fifty epithets into the match, Ebenezer interrupts them, misnaming them once again ("Ladies! Ladies!"), and the women, laughing, ignore him and continue. Another eighty insults pass before he is able to speak again, and this time he "commands" them to stop (in the first edition of the novel, he is by now so weakened and overwhelmed by this barrage that he is "reeling" about the room). The name-calling continues, and two and a half pages later Ebenezer flings his own insult ("Foul-mouthed harridans!") at the women before fleeing through the door by which he entered (441–47).

Ebenezer's weaknesses are all on display in this section. Unable to pierce Joan Toast's disguise, he dismisses her even as she attempts to guide him, thereby losing both her aid and an opportunity to be reunited with the woman he loves. When his search for her becomes embroiled in the whores' debate, his ineffectual attempts to end the match result in his leaving before gaining any useful information from them. Finally, his tendency to run from place to place without reflection betrays him: he reaches the relative peace and quiet of William Smith's company and then allows Smith to dupe him into the marriage contract which is the final validation of the loss of his family estate, Malden.

That this marriage is to Susan Warren, or rather Joan Toast—the woman above all (with the exception perhaps of his own sister Anna) whom Ebenezer would *wish* to marry—can be of little comfort to Ebenezer, for the Joan Toast who gave up whoring to follow him to Maryland is now poxed and

addicted to opium. Stripping the disguise will be a bitter reve-
lation for Ebenezer; out of all the names for whore shouted back
and forth in the halls of Malden, he failed to hear the one that
will have the most meaning for him: wife.

In the first edition of *The Sot-Weed Factor,* Ebenezer's reaction to the whores' contest is extraordinarily violent: he covers
his ears and reels "about the room as if each epithet were a blow
to the head" (469). This reaction is muted in the revised
version, but one might still find it intriguing that the Laureate
refuses the linguistic challenge implicit in the whores' game,
particularly since language games have pleased him so
much in the past. The first chapter of the novel recounts the
language games Ebenezer played with his twin sister, Anna:
vocabulary games, rhyming contests, "elaborate codes, reverse
pronunciations, and home-made languages" (6). Later, while
traveling with Henry Burlingame, Ebenezer matches Hudibras-
tic verse with Burlingame and delights in instructing his former
tutor in this new form of linguistic play.[4]

The linguistic play with Anna is a bonding experience; the
words the twins share in the dark bring them close together. The
later experience also begins as an attempt to bond, for Ebenezer and Burlingame have been divided by Burlingame's cru-
elty to Father Smith at Island Creek. A discussion of poetry and
the rhyming game remove the tension of that division by divert-
ing Ebenezer's attention away from his loss of faith in Burlingame and toward his involvement in (and eventual loss of)
the contest. However, Ebenezer finds the linguistic play
at Malden to be an experience of exclusion. Here, he stands
outside the game, watching in frustration as the whores are
united in mock battle. His attempts at interruption are not aimed
at gaining entrance to the game but at ending the game; he
wants information from the women, not pleasure or union.

Ebenezer has no immediate interest in the content of the list
that evolves; the synonyms for "whore" block his attempts to
control the conversation by guiding it toward information-
exchange behavior. He thus experiences the list as noise rather

than as information or as play. The list is neither pleasurable nor useful, and his one desire is to end it. He effectually accomplishes this by leaving the room, but in doing so he sacrifices access to information; the whores might have been able to tell him about Susan Warren.

In truth, Susan Warren is a whore like the ones engaging in the debate. That the Gargantuan list is comprised of names that *all* apply to this one woman—under her real name the object of Ebenezer's love, and under her assumed name the object of his search—is nicely ironic. It also mirrors the excess of names attached to the males in the novel; in Ebenezer's experience thus far, names have been peculiarly slippery and overabundant, and it may be that this excess of naming now repels him.[5] In any case, both versions of the novel portray him as resentful of the whores, angry that they ignore him and resist his attempts to impose order upon them.

Ebenezer loses control of the dialogue immediately after initiating it. He is pushed aside as the women begin to feed epithets back and forth to each other with no regard for the man whose inquiry set them in motion. He is excluded, placed outside the discourse of sexual experience, marked by his non-participation in this game just as he is marked throughout the novel by his alleged innocence. The whores form a unit during their engagement in this naming ritual; they are bonded by their acknowledgment of these names—which Bakhtin would call "nicknames" and describe as inherently evaluative (1984, 459)—and their acknowledgment defuses the abusiveness of the names and makes them appellations of mirth and membership.[6] They thus turn inward toward their own sex and society, ironically gaining "mastery" of this situation by playing with names they acquired by reason of their very failure to exclude men from their intercourse.

Ebenezer is excluded from this dialogue in other ways. Although he is a poet, the women's wall of language is so dense that he is not able to penetrate it. His linguistically pallid "ladies, ladies" does not even rate recognition from the combatants; eventually he calls them "harridans," a minimally respectable addition to the dictionary being compiled here, but only as he flees the field.[7] Had he been able (or had he permitted himself) to join in the fray, this might have been a significant turning point, for a *free* (rather than coerced or gulled) participation in the world of the grotesque might have revealed to him the true nature of Maryland and his role there.

As it is, he flees knowledge as he flees the room. Sexual competency supports the whores' linguistic capability, and this combination threatens a contamination the innocent Ebenezer cannot endure. In his "Paean to Purity" he had proclaimed his belief that a fall from innocence would mean a loss of protection from "Life, from Time, from Death, from History" (59). However, by the time he encounters the three whores, Ebenezer is completely involved in the creation of History in Maryland and now genuinely faces Death because of the "seasoning" sickness. So this overwhelming list that not only names whores but suggests that there are many ways of becoming a whore simply makes mockery of his attempts to retain the protection of innocence. Eventually, in a brilliant textual maneuver, the young man is literally driven off the page by the voices of experience.

Hipkiss, in *The American Absurd,* suggests that Barth's narrative intricacies and linguistic play are "merely decorative" (1984, 112); although few other critics would go so far, the six-page list of "whores" is generally more noted for its virtuosity and comprehensiveness than for its strategic potential. However, I would insist that this extraordinary list is located at a narrative crux: within thirty pages of Ebenezer's flight from the whores, he has married Susan Warren and sealed the loss of Malden, he has recovered from the seasoning sickness and penned "The Sot-Weed Factor," he has discovered that Susan Warren is in fact Joan Toast, and he has left Joan Toast whoring with the Indians to gain passage money to England while he runs away into the night. The second section of the novel ends here, with Ebenezer's utter degradation; the third, in which he finally "earns" Malden, is ready to begin.

In addition, the list names the structure of the novel, for *The Sot-Weed Factor* is indeed framed and guided by whores. Ebenezer's first separation from twin sister Anna is marked by Burlingame's visit to a brothel; Ebenezer's journey to Maryland is precipitated by the wager that sends Joan Toast away, unswived and unpaid; Ebenezer's first encounter with temptation (and rape) occurs when the whoreship *Cyprian* is overtaken by Ebenezer's captors and his second occurs when he attempts to overpower Susan Warren and then arranges to meet her in the barn; Mary Mungommory, the Traveling Whore of Dorset, twice aids Ebenezer, and the tale of her sister Katy (the Seagoing Whore of Dorset) is intimately linked to Burlingame's quest for a father; Malden is turned into a brothel; Ebenezer describes his "Marylandiad" (later "The Sot-Weed Factor") as a scourge to lash Maryland with as "a harlot is scourged at the public post, [to] catalogue her every wickedness" (458); Burlingame suggests that every advancement he has gained has been earned by sexual favors (331); and every woman in the novel is a fallen woman, from Ebenezer's nursemaid to his twin sister, Anna, whose sexual adventures with Burlingame and Billy Rumbly leave her (like her twin) a mere "technical" virgin.

In the end, Ebenezer's life is punctuated by one last whore when he chooses to warn against Fame in his epitaph, calling her "a fickle Slut, and whory" (756). As distinctions collapse or are mutually embraced throughout the novel, the opposition of whore and not-whore seems at first to be the only one remaining, and this final accusation of "Fame" appears to confirm the strength of the whore/not-whore polarity. However, like the virtually nonexistent "virgin," the class "not-whore" is, in *The Sot-Weed Factor,* a null set. All the characters are whores in one sense or another, and—just as it does in the list—the appellation "whore" loses force as a term of abuse in the face of this universality.

Clearly, the list of "whores" is no mere linguistic flourish; it is a functional hyposystem in *The Sot-Weed Factor* supersystem. Its systemically symmetrical structure repeats and reinforces systemic concerns with ordering processes, nominative procedure, and oppositional definition. As a node occupying space in the narratological subsystem, it interacts with and is realized by the artifactual subsystem whose function is representation. As an agent of the narrative system, it responds to and constrains the operations of the reader system, whose function is interpretation.

Textually, a space for interaction is created by the aggressively columnar nature of the list. The surrounding blocks of text are virtually forced apart, making the reader witness to a visual penetration of the narrative. This penetration, or disruption, is emphasized by the white border surrounding this columnar text; the interruption of the traditional paragraph-to-paragraph flow of narrative marks the essential difference, the listness, of this textual object while it calls the reader's attention to the artifactual and strategic nature of the list.

This particular list's verticality works both textually and thematically. Its columnar nature makes it readily available to the eye; it has more presence as a list than if it were contained in a block paragraph (as, say, the *Gatsby* list is), since its form can immediately be recognized as "list." The reader, prepared by ordering conventions, is immediately aware that the page contains a number of linked items. Further, the eye moves easily up and down a column. Such a list can be skimmed so that the words fly by as in a rapid exchange of speech—here, mirroring the events taking place in the narrative. Finally, it seems at least not inappropriate that a list about whores would be long, upright, and straight: an erection of words.[8] Since the phallus is precisely linked (conventionally, if not actually) to the creation of the class "whore," its presence in the representation of this list serves as a nice social symbol that is only minimally obscured from the reader's vision.[9]

Focus and distance are problems inherent in the reader's relationship to the text. She is inevitably aware of her distance from the narrative: a book (or other technological artifact) holds the words of the narrative, and the reader's physical relationship to that artifact reminds her of its contained and exclusive nature. Thus her control of the linguistic material in the narrative appears cybernetically limited to interpretive (or reading) strategies and to acts of violence against the physical artifact itself (she could, for instance, rip out a page). Barth, in the construction of his Gargantuan, bilingual list of synonyms for "whore," seems to emphasize the reader's exclusion from the writing process; the very comprehensiveness of the list ought perhaps to suggest to the reader that creative participation in this naming is no longer possible. However, the design of the list-making process *within* the narrative is one of challenge, in this case a contest between informed participants. A similar structure of challenge exists between Barth and the reader; the reader is implicitly invited to add to the list and the generous white border provides room to do so.[10]

The list further serves as a focal point for the reader's struggle for textual authority. Barth has used *two* languages in the compilation of the lists. Therefore, only a reader with a truly intimate knowledge of French can participate fully in the reading of the list; others must accept Barth's authority, relying upon his command of French. The position of this latter group seems rather precarious; as monolingual readers, they must accept some one hundred "whores" as potentially nonsensical. A resistance to Barth's authority in this matter thus creates a gap; the reader must place the French "whores" outside the space of accepted information. On the other hand, the reader may *choose* to submit to Barth's linguistic power; and, like the thrill inherent in the threat of the self-generating list, a certain gratification may be found in this act of willing submission: indeed, sadomasochistic principles suggest that a giving up of control in the face of power (and in the realm of excess) provides particular pleasure.

It is possible for the reader's response to the list of "whores" to be expressed in silence, a refusal to add to the already excessive list, a reluctance to debate issues of authority. The list itself may, by its very concern with noise, suggest that silence is a critical issue. Indeed, Ihab Hassan believes that the postmodern movement as a whole may be represented as an impulse toward silence; in *The Dismemberment of Orpheus,* he identifies silence as his "metaphor of a language that expresses . . . the stress in art, culture, and consciousness" (1982, 12). Silence, then, is a language of excess ending in an exhaustion of possibilities, of too many words leading to no more words; silence, then, is the language of the unspeakable and of the spoken that is beyond recall. In the voice of the list maker, it is a language that expresses the failure of information to be contained or containable.

Under the stress of exhausted possibilities, Barth's list of synonyms for "whore" pushes the word toward silence, whether it be the silence of fulfillment or the silence of despair. Hassan calls Barth's silences (engendered by exhaustion) those of "waiters upon transcendence" (1982, 251). He suggests that the replenishment Barth seeks (of form, of the word, of history) is achieved by a mystical faith, that through negation and exhaustion, one might come to renewal. Visually, the space around Barth's list of "whores" is a space of separation, of distance, and of loss; in that margin, it would seem that no voice speaks unless it be the voice of the reader. The list appears to leave the whores standing apart, textually isolated, framed by block paragraphs that mark the end of their game. However, a frame suggests that what is enclosed is an object meriting heightened attention; by this framing, Barth creates an environment in which the *next* word might be heard.[11]

E. P. Walkiewicz suggests that the list of synonyms, exhausted by the whores and replenished by Ebenezer's "harridans," is exemplary of Barth's theory about the cyclical structure of narration and is "designed to foster the belief that the text is characterized everywhere else by a similar cyclic process of replenishment—exhaustion—replenishment . . ." (1986, 49). This cycle is indeed represented in an earlier list. In this scene (which takes place prior to Ebenezer's embarkation for Maryland) Ebenezer attempts to purchase a notebook for his poetry. Benjamin Bragg's list of the "species of common notebooks" (110) available at his shop pushes Eben-ezer Cooke into a rage at this unnecessary complication of life by a plethora of options. The list takes four oppositions (thin/fat, plain/ruled, cardboard/leather, and quarto/folio) and drives them to the limits of their combinatorial possibilities.[12] Eben-ezer, unable to choose among the sixteen alternatives, refuses to compromise and ends by stealing the stationer's own note-book and fleeing the premises. Like Ebenezer's addition to the dictionary of abuse created by the whores, his replenishment of notebook options permits him to move forward in the narrative. However, in this case he has truly replenished an exhausted set because he has chosen an item from outside the definition and forced it to be available to him.

The list engendered by Bragg's exercise in combinatorial logic is one in which each item is utterly unlike all the others, even though they are constructed from the same set of oppo-sitions. The challenge presented by such a list is not that of addition (as in the list of synonyms) but of subtraction: to re-move the *one* notebook from the set which is most suitable, desirable, useful, or, perhaps, most representative of a chosen notebook ideology. The difficulty of this task paralyzes Eben-ezer: he is a character who cannot choose and cannot compro-mise. He eventually finds his release from paralysis in changing the terms of the problem, making it one of addition (to the set) *and* subtraction (of the notebook from the premises). Ironically, the notebook he steals is a hybrid, "quarto size, about an inch thick, with cardboard covers and a leather spine" (113) and has already been used to keep the stationer's accounts. Ebenezer rips out Bragg's accounts and appropriates the blank pages for his own use.

Another example of such a replenishment might be found in a list that is itself an emblem of plenitude. One of the docu-ments circulating throughout *The Sot-Weed Factor* is John Smith's *Secret Historie,* which recounts Smith's journey up the Chesapeake Bay with his rival, Lord Henry Burlingame, the grandfather of tutor Henry Burlingame III. One section of this

journal (discovered when Ebenezer falls into the hands of se-
ditious natives) details the manner by which the savage Ahatchwhoops choose a leader. Contenders for leadership, or their
appointed proxies, prove their superiority in a battle of bellies;
the greatest glutton becomes king on the theory that "the more
a man can eat, the bigger he will become, and the heavier there
King, the more secure will be there towne, against its enemies"
(560). In the journal, Smith gleefully reports that he has maneu-
vered Burlingame into serving as proxy for one of the contenders for the Ahatchwhoop throne;[13] a victory by Burlingame at
table will thus mean co-leadership of the Ahatchwhoops, ne-
cessitating (Smith believes) Burlingame's remaining with the
savages for the remainder of his life.

The feast set before the gluttons is noted down by Smith in
a list, the "summe of what they eat" (563). He records the name
and amount of each item consumed, as well as the manner in
which the items were killed or prepared:

> Of snypes, one apiece, bagg'd.
> Of black & white warblers, one apiece,
>   throttl'd.
> Of rubie-throated hummingbirds, two
>   apiece, scalded, pickl'd, & intensify'd.
> . . . .
> Of *raccoon,* half a one apiece, grutted.
> Of dogg, equal portions, a sort of spaniell
>   it was.
> Of venison, one pryme apiece, dry'd.
> . . . .
> No rabbitts. (563–64)

The gluttons feast upon the listed items, matching each
other bite for bite, until the native contender expires; Smith
urges Burlingame to swallow once more, since a tie is not a
victory in this contest. Burlingame refuses, and the selection of
a King is held in suspension until Smith takes "the last boyl'd
batt" from the cauldron and thrusts it into Burlingame's mouth;

Smith thumps Burlingame on the head, the bat goes down, and Burlingame is declared co-ruler of the Ahatchwhoops (with native Wepenter, for whom he served as proxy[14]) and is left behind by Smith and his company.

Smith's action—like Ebenezer's theft of the stationer's notebook—falls outside the parameters of the challenge. Nowhere in the construction of the contest is it indicated that noncombatants might intrude into the arena of the feast to force-feed the gluttons. In the context of the challenge, the action is completed: the native has eaten himself to death, and Burlingame is unable to continue on his own volition. The list, too, is completed; since it is constituted by items eaten, it must necessarily end when the gluttons refuse additional food. Curiously, the list (and the narrative) is renewed not by the addition of a fresh item but by the reintroduction of a previously rejected item, a leftover bat. When Smith forces the bat into Burlingame's mouth, he simultaneously replenishes the challenge and the list while affirming the comprehensive nature of the feast as an encyclopedia of foods available in Maryland.

This list foregrounds the extraordinary abundance of colonial Maryland; it is indeed a self-giving land, in which none need go hungry. That Ebenezer Cooke spends much of the novel surviving on scant rations simply strengthens his portrayal as a stranger to the great world: one who rejects his carnal nature and who is alien to the notion of abundance. In contrast, Henry Burlingame III's grandfather quite literally *eats* the world, he consumes Maryland. The grandson's inclusive nature, his tendency to swallow the world, is a legacy from this Gargantuan predecessor.

Bakhtin links banquets and feasts to an identification with the "devoured and devouring" world (1984, 221); in the presence of food, and in the consumption of food, we acknowledge our dependence upon the regenerative cycle of life: birth, death, decay, rebirth. Thus, Bakhtin suggests, every feast is an affirmation of renewal. The feast recounted in Smith's *Secret Historie* is just such a celebration: the loss of the old ruler is confirmed by and assuaged by this participation in ceremony; food is consumed, prolongs life, and is excreted onto a newly fertile earth; an assumption of continued abundance is announced by the ready consumption of goods on hand; and the new king is physically symbolic of the continuity of the natural order.

The structure of the feast confirms a foraging pattern, one expressive of the relative difficulty of obtaining game; seafood is served first, then fowl, and finally the meats. Smith's list duplicates the overall structure of the feast, inserting an internal enumerative structure that expands upon and details the consumptive end of the foraging process. However, some items having distinct culinary identities (and which may have been consumed separately) are recorded generically. These groupings make it impossible to count the actual number of different items served: for example, Smith lists "such other sea-food as the greate Baye doth give up" and "divers eggs." The implied necessity of such groupings suggests an even greater abundance than is documented in the list itself.[15]

On the other hand, the negation in Smith's account—"No rabbitts"—implies a significant absence. That such a common (and easily caught) creature should *not* be served at this apparently comprehensive banquet calls our attention to the symbolic import of the rabbit: it is an emblem of fertility, of endlessly fecund sexual activity. Lord Burlingame's minuscule penis (and stunned and glutted state) prevents him from performing his first kingly duty, the impregnation of the old king's wife, and it may therefore not be inappropriate to read this absent rabbit as prefiguring Burlingame's impotence.

In light of this inability, this inactivity, the dynamic nature of the hunting and/or culinary terminology in the list gains a certain resonance. Smith reports that the game is "dry'd, boyl'd, frizzl'd, blow'd, stew'd, pouder'd, scalded, pickl'd, intensify'd, crack'd, dyc'd, smother'd, fry'd, roasted" and "spitted & turn'd" after being "bagg'd, throttl'd, bill'd, growsl'd, disembowell'd, fetch'd, and grutted" (collated from 563).[16] This dynamism, attached to foodstuffs, is a reversal of the

Hippocratic anthology Bakhtin sees in Rabelais's enumeration of eliminative processes (1984, 357–58); in Barth's list the nutrients have a rich verbal life *before* they pass into the alimentary system. While the enumerations themselves are celebratory of both consumption and generation, Barth's enumeration ironically leads directly to a *failure* of generative force.

Lord Burlingame's physical handicap forces him to resort to the Rite of the Sacred Eggplant in order to procreate;[17] Henry Burlingame III's identical handicap leads him to embrace a wealth of sexual activities and partners before finally resorting to the eggplant himself. He is a self-described "Husband to all Creation" (497) and thus serves in the novel as a representative of universal carnal knowledge. This descendant of the devourer of the world—who also names himself the "Embracer of Contradictories"—is thus uniquely positioned to educate Ebenezer about the generative force symbolized by united twins.

Twins are a living contradiction: united in the womb and forever separate in the world, they symbolize for Burlingame the human urge to coalesce (489), to return all oppositions to a state of synthesis. Burlingame's compendium of twin lore (which is, in effect, a chapter-long list) thus serves not only as a showcase for Barth's erudition (as Stark suggests in *The Literature of Exhaustion* [1974, 149]), but as a disquisition on the inevitable collapse of polarity. For Burlingame, the binary oppositions represented in global twin mythology tend toward collapse and union in the implied desire of one twin for the other. His own desire, expressed in this chapter, is to mate with the united twins; as "Suitor of Totality" he will then be able to join himself with the token of the "seamless universe" (497).

If a failure of binarism is implied in Barth's twin lore, then differentiation and opposition cannot be relied upon to keep order in the world. A tendency toward reconciliation, toward union, means instability of borders and barriers: an instability of ordering devices. Even achieved synthesis holds danger. Burlingame's desire for a seamless universe is an apocalyptic one; such a universe implies a stasis, or at the very least a rebirth from the ashes of binarism.

Perhaps it is apocalypse that is suggested in the "comic order" created by "exhaustiveness for its own sake" (Joseph 1970, 29). If words wind down to stasis, or to silence, then the next moment must indeed be a revelatory one: either of a true end to narrative or of a renewal. But the exhaustiveness itself, before the moment of apocalypse, participates in its own order, the order of comprehensive knowledge.

Lists that offer an exhaustion of potential, the inclusion of all the members of a set, suggest that there is an inherent value in this sort of ordering of information. However, Ebenezer's paralysis in the face of alternatives (such as the notebook options) seems to contradict this. Like other Barth characters who suffer from cosmopsis, Ebenezer is overwhelmed by options or alternatives; action depends upon the ability to choose among options or to distinguish the meaningful from the meaningless, and Ebenezer's inaction points to the inadequacy of free facts. Barth's twin lore obviously privileges knowledge over ignorance, but it also suggests that knowledge itself is useless, paralytic—simply held in potential until some other ordering process is performed upon it.

Burlingame's discourse on twins claims a comprehensive knowledge of the subject; because Ebenezer is himself part of the information, the entire discourse is relevant to him and linked intimately to his state of being. But order is not imposed on this conglomeration of facts until later, when Burlingame provides an interpretive framework for it. Until then, the twin lore has the same order as the world: "everything that is the case."[18]

The postmodern novel seems concerned with negotiating a position from which to narrate everything that is the case and to examine the tales created from selected items of that Gargantuan list that is the past. Hayden White suggests that history, as a narrative form, is closely linked to list making; medieval *annals,* he notes, record events and years without commentary, but the "'meaning' of the events is their registration in this kind of list" (1981, 9): the implied importance of the recorded items gives them the quality of narrative. Further, as an ordering device, the historical account is intimately linked to the processes we use to create lists: classification, categorization, selection, and interpretive framing. Barth, in constructing a historical novel that is so heavily dependent upon lists as a narrative device, seems to ask for a reexamination, not only of the novel as a narrative form, but of our very notion of history as knowable and narratable.

Robert Scholes sees a distinctly historical trend in post–World War II novels when he notes that

> North American works [such as *The Sot-Weed Factor* and *Gravity's Rainbow*], in particular, bristle with facts and smell of research of the most painstaking kind. Yet they deliberately challenge the notion that history may be retrieved by objective investigations of fact. (1979, 207)

Assuming that an objective investigation of fact is even possible, how does one jump the gap between history and fact? Barth seems to suggest that the gap is in reality an abyss; that no amount of facts, and no one interpretive framework, can bridge such a chasm. And while *The Sot-Weed Factor* extolls the attractiveness, the desirability of synthesis, in the end the novel implies that no such synthesis is possible, that much as the poles yearn to merge, any union is temporary and tainted by the gall of achieved desire.

Ultimately, for Barth, the chronicle is suspect; history is somehow more and less than fact. *The Sot-Weed Factor* fairly trumpets the unreliability of historical documentation and identification; moreover, it foregrounds the essentially grotesque and (at least potentially) fictive nature of temporal cause and effect. Barth reveals to us a past that is merely a chaotic list of characters and events from which we cull a narrative we call "history," in a highly arbitrary and individualistic selection process that is not even limited by truth. For Barth, the history of Maryland—like Ebenezer Cooke—is available and open to all comers: one more whore in virgin territory.

Perhaps Barth's novel does not itself replenish that exhausted whore we call History. But by pushing the historical account (along with the list and the novel) to the very limits of its capacity, he at least calls our attention to the feeble state of those narratives we have heretofore called "history"—and perhaps creates a space where the next narrative can be inscribed.

In Raymond Mazurek's estimation, *The Sot-Weed Factor* is a structuralist, narrativized reading of history that owes much to the influence of the Pax Americana of the 1950s and 1960s: it begins by establishing adventuresome alternatives (enumerating the stories) and ends by valorizing moderation (1985, 73–77). And it is certainly true that in the notebook scene, Peter Sayer (Henry Burlingame in disguise) does advise a selection based on the Golden Mean. However, Mazurek's evaluation seems to me to reduce Barth's multidirectional effort to a disappointingly mundane caution against excess. An interpretation more consistent with Barth's notions of replenishment would be that the social narrative must move through moderation and balance[19] and into the realm of endured chaos. Here, in the maelstrom of historico-linguistic alternatives, elements can be examined, selected, and recombined into new patterns and a temporary (and arbitrary) order can be created.

Inside the List

*Any classification is superior to chaos
and even a classification at the level
of sensible properties is a step toward
rational ordering.*

—*Claude Lévi-Strauss*
The Savage Mind

All systems are essentially contingent; structures that are dependent upon relationality for morphology have a tenuous spatiotemporal existence. Even when fixed by a text, narrative systems seem threatened, prone to alteration of significance if not form, subject to alternative interpretation even when relational formations have been maintained over extended periods of time. No position inside the narrative supersystem is entirely stable, no structure is completely solid, and thus the security of systemic activities relies on chaos-management techniques up and down the scale of operations.

Located deep within the narrative supersystem, a hyposystem is a basal structure, perhaps the smallest unit functioning above the level of grammar. Individual narratological substructures inhabit this region, the site of actualization for the narratological subsystem; here, substructures or hyposystems realize the strategy that constitutes and constructs narrative. At this scale of systemic operation, hyposystems channel narrative energy from point to point within the strategic structure and link component nodes together, forming and stating a relational collective that will be textualized in the artifactual subsystem. In addition, the hyposystems contain and transfer specific narratological information, providing locations where difference and distinction are recorded and spaces where sameness and association may finally be significant.

As a hyposystemic entity, the list, a formally and conceptually systematized block of information, interacts with other narratological units in the instantiation of an overall narrative strategy. It functions systematically, maintaining its own structural integrity in the face of environmental perturbation and incorporating new information as an impetus for change and growth. At the same time, it engages in and echoes the dialogue between chaos and order that whispers in the background of all systemic endeavors. Indeed, by its very nature a list comments upon the opposition between order and disorder, rendering categorical assumptions visible and participating in the enforcement of local regulation even when its structural fissures provide an entry for chaotic material.

As a chaos-management operation, the list works to impose order on even the most contentious material. In the human system, for instance, the brain

> looks for ways to lower the entropy of a collection of items by reducing the number of ways in which they can be arranged. . . . If the items display no obvious relationships, no discernible pattern, the brain will invent relationships, imposing some arbitrary order on the disorderliness of the material. A list of items in which each item is independent of all the others is just noise. (Hofstadter 1979, 215–16)

Thus, even an arbitrary order imposed on entropic data depends upon systematization, upon relational networks that arrange substantive components into a systemically functional coalition.

The resultant structure reveals and actualizes those relations, and the fact that the relations are contrived rather than natural does not invalidate the structure; it stands, within its systemic environment, as securely as one built upon the most stable and obvious of datic relations. Until the imposed relations weaken, this act of chaos management is as effective as any other.

Clearly, an assumption underlying the construction of lists is that order can be imposed upon (or revealed within) any aggregation of objects or events, that the natural tendency of separate entities toward chaos can in fact be reversed by a declaration of relation.[1] On the level of information, that relational structure separates the ordered from the unordered, forming a container around a group of class members united by a categorical coherence and a fundamental epistemological integrity. In terms of the system, though, the distinction between order and disorder is a dynamic process that establishes the list's identity and simultaneously enables filtration and absorption procedures, border fortification or restructuration, and component positioning—activities that ensure the longevity of or the integrity of the system as it interacts with a chaotic environment.

Borges's famous Chinese encyclopedia foregrounds the problem of chaotic intrusions into categorization or list construction processes. This list seems a relatively simple statement of class division; it declares that

> animals are divided into: (a) belonging to the Emperor, (b) embalmed, (c) tame, (d) sucking pigs, (e) sirens, (f) fabulous, (g) stray dogs, (h) included in the present classification, (i) frenzied, (j) innumerable, (k) drawn with a very fine camelhair brush, (l) *et cetera,* (m) having just broken the water pitcher, (n) that from a long way off look like flies. (quoted in Foucault 1973, xv)[2]

However, an analysis of the intrasystemic relations expressed here suggests that a disturbing element has entered into the structural process: a metacategorical statement—item (h), "included in the present classification"—subsumes all other members into its own position even as it preserves a visual and spatial equivalence with the other positions in the structure. When item (l) is sucked down into this systemic black hole, item (h) swells to an incredible (and unrepresentable) size, extending the relatively concise itemization Borges has offered toward infinity, an action which subverts both the categorization function and the containment function of the list.[3]

Locating the list's chaotic potential in a conceptual disjunction, Foucault finds that Borges's list does violence to our notions of *how* things may be ordered. In his analysis, he notes that in

> the wonderment of this taxonomy . . . [what] is
> demonstrated as the exotic charm of another
> system of thought, is the limitation of our own,
> the stark impossibility of thinking *that*.
> (1973, xv)

Here, he implies that our own classificatory processes, our discourse or linguistic structures, and our cultural and epistemological assumptions have us conceptually bound and that any transgression of our established classificatory boundaries is cognitively disruptive, threatening the security of conventional thought. Borges disturbs us because he crosses the border into the region of the uncategorical category. This violation of procedure is facilitated by the plasticity of the list format, since lists can stretch and contract at need in the accommodation of awkward class members. However, the full empowerment of Borges's project comes primarily from a misapplication of categorical construction codes which allows him to build a logical edifice that threatens to collapse if an apparent internal coherence is privileged over a dynamic (and necessarily unstable) structuration.

Foucault insists that *only in language* can a site be created where Borges's listed categories can coexist, that there is no other space where they can be juxtaposed as a logical series. This site lies outside the terms of normal relations or normal taxonomy, within a spatial paradigm or "heterotopia" that permits constructions based on difference and disorder.[4] Curiously, however, language also controls the chaotic effect of such a juxtaposition, since the conceptual disorder threatened by the Borges list is to some degree limited or even defused by linguistic sanitation; the mediation of language distances class members from the organizing intelligence and from each other, and this decontamination through decontextualization minimizes the turbulent potential of "unthinkable" categories.

Perhaps there are no genuinely unthinkable categories; Claude Lévi-Strauss points out that "each 'local' logic exists in its own right [and] consists in the intelligibility of the relation between two immediately associated terms . . . (1966, 161). In other words, the logic of categories is local and contingent rather than universal or objective, and thus it need not be consistent across categories. Indeed, research indicates that classificatory logic is often not even consistent *within* categories.

In his comprehensive work on categorization, *Women, Fire, and Dangerous Things,* George Lakoff opposes an "experientialist" theory of categories to classical objectivist theories which do not acknowledge the organic origin of thought. Lakoff contends that categorical construction is an act of creation rather than a simple representation of preexisting relations. When examined in the light of new research and new theory, the category is revealed as a dynamic structure that functions systemically; a gestalt entity constituted by relational configurations, the category embodies physical and social experience as it interacts ecologically with other thought structures (1987, xiv–xv).

In Lakoff's theoretical conception of cognitive structuration, internal organizations of information lead to the development of "idealized cognitive models," which in turn lead to the construction of categories. Propositional models specify members, properties, and relations, just as Carraway's categorization of party guests does. An image-schematic model, on the other hand, is structured by movement or shape, the way a shopping list maps the structure of the store or a class cluster models a trajectory or physical linkage. Metaphoric models map similarities between one conceptual domain and another, and metonymic ones associate properties so that one function of a member comes to represent a property conforming to selection principles, enabling entry to the class for an otherwise dissimilar member (Lakoff 1987, 113–44).

The categories themselves have certain fundamental principles of construction which affect the selection of members as well as the configuration of the cognitive model. An important principle is that of *centrality,* the existence of central members in a class. *Chaining* extends a class through linkage to the central member, depending on basic culture-specific regions of experience known as *experiential domains* for codes that allow chain formation even when connections are otherwise obscure or contrary to conventional classification. The process described here is essentially organic, one of growth and extension under construction codes that are locally determined. These principles of construction directly contradict classical theories about category formation, which insist that categories are imposed upon classes defined by objective properties rather than by other sorts of relation.

Specialized knowledge tends to prevail over general knowledge in category formation; specific information about a class member can qualify it for inclusion in a class to which it would not ordinarily belong or exclude it from a class to which more general information would otherwise assign it. However, even a great deal of information about the principles that *motivate* (make sense of) a category does not make prediction of future class members possible; categorization and model construction can be fully understood only in retrospect, after the process of creation has taken place (Lakoff 1987, 95–96).

Eleanor Rosch's conception of the categorical prototype grows out of experiments that reveal a series of asymmetrical functions centering around the "best example" of a class. In interactions with individual class members inside categories, experimental subjects exhibit graded perceptions of similarity, variant reaction or recognition times, and differential generalization of new information to class members (Lakoff 1987, 41). Rosch finds that in each category, one member—the prototype—can be singled out as the most representative member of the class or as the one which best matches the qualification constellation that patterns the class; that prototype is more quickly recognized as a class member than others and less likely to have negative information about the class generalized to it.

The prototype of "guests at Gatsby's parties" may actually be Nick Carraway himself. Carraway's own name, although implicitly included rather than explicitly enumerated, certainly informs the category he creates; indeed, his integral relation to the classification process suggests that he qualifies as the best example of his class: the guest most consistently in attendance, best able to identify and rank others, and nearest to the source of patterning motivation.[5] He even escapes the negative generalization he applies to the other members of the class, that they accept "Gatsby's hospitality and [pay] him the subtle tribute of knowing nothing whatever about him" (61). Carraway accepts Gatsby's hospitality but is not passively parasitic; rather he engages in an active investigation and analysis of his host, a difference that is verified by his central role in the construction and inscription of this very category.

Many categories are formed by the influence of a framing structure, normally an activity or contingent event, rather than by member similarity (Lakoff 1987, 21). The "party guest" category is one of these; its frame is a spatiotemporal one, defined by Gatsby's parties and not by any overt likeness among the individuals on the list. However, inside this frame subcategories do form around certain member similarities, and these are represented in Carraway's construction of the list. He chooses place of origin as the principal property for clustering or subcategory formation.[6] The internal structure of the enumeration is framed by a succession of place names. Secondary subcategories form around occupational or behavioral similarities and are expressed semantically and (occasionally) by contiguity. The film people, the theatrical people, and the men who gamble at the parties, for instance, are clustered on the page as well as within a conceptual frame.

An analysis of the list's construction suggests a categorical hierarchy[7] based upon the level of Carraway's own information about the guests. That hierarchy might be represented as follows:

GENERAL   potential guest, not attending (0)
                attending but not observed by
                    Carraway (0)
                named party guest
                    (the list: 66 members)
                guest/identified by origin (66)
                guest/origin/additional information (36)
SPECIFIC   guest/origin/2 types of information (4)

However, this hierarchization is a representation of Carraway's ordering of the category; it does not inform the creation of the category itself and has nothing to do with the *selection* of class members. It speaks to the further or more precise identification of members who have already been selected into the category by their presence (or right to be present) at the party. In effect, this hierarchy is a series of informational frames, leading inward toward a center of highest information (per guest) from an external boundary occupied by the invisible guests about whom no information is available. Rather than marking some distinction relating to class membership, the frame controls an internal ordering process; it is a chaos-management technique that prevents a large and potentially unruly class from settling into random order.

Magnitude has an inevitably chaotic effect; an over-populated category threatens to collapse into disorder or to insist upon arbitrary subformations that subvert the representational intent of the category itself. Formal subclasses contain the entropic tendencies of ordered data, putting another layer of structure between the central order and excentric chaos. In addition, the act of sorting concentrates value and potential energy in these subsets (Paulson 1988, 41). Once clustering establishes intercomponent coherence, a subset can interact dynamically with other clusters at a systemic level one step above that of the individual member.

Although most of the subsets within Carraway's list work to clarify and solidify his categorical structure, refining the identification process he initiates, one subset has precisely the opposite effect. Nested within the category "party guests" is a small subset (containing six members) which might be labeled "party guests with adjuncts." This chaotic subset questions the integrity of Carraway's construction process by violating the premises upon which his classification is erected. Further, its continuing existence within that space of violation validates (by default) a subversively uncategorical category.

The presence of adjuncts is noted in two ways, either during naming or during the provision of guest history.[8] These are people who either come with party guests or who interact with them at the party and who are not otherwise named: Beluga's nameless "girls"; Mrs. Ulysses Swett, who runs over Snell's hand; Etty, the bum who fights with Clarence Endive; the nameless man reputed to be Miss Claudia Hip's chauffeur; and Benny McClenahan's four almost identical (but always different, though certainly interchangeable) girls, whose names might be "Jacqueline . . . or else Consuela, or Gloria or Judy or June . . ." (63).

The adjuncts enter the party (and thus the list) by association, forming a nebulous underclass within the structure enclosing legitimate guests. The guests are always quite specifically identified; the adjuncts, however, drift about in a cloud of imprecise information, often nameless and always attached to statements about chance, conflict, or inaccuracy. Their presence disrupts the orderly construction of Carraway's list, acting as an internal perturbation, a chaotic intrusion into the structuration process. First, the adjuncts problematize Carraway's decision to *name* the guests: Beluga's girls have no names at all, and neither does the chauffeur; Benny McClenahan's girls might have the names Carraway provides but also might not. In addition, the adjuncts interfere with an accurate head count: the number of Beluga's girls is not given, and McClenahan's girls have indefinite multiples, since the number of *sets* of different girls is never indicated. Ultimately, the presence of this underclass deforms the categorical structure, which purports to list the party guests but is unable to do so precisely because of this shifting subset.

The adjunct subset is a paradoxical site much like item (h) in Borges's Chinese encyclopedia, an unstable class position within a systematization of class; the subset thus requires an alteration of, or an indefinite suspension of, categorical premises. Further, this disorderly unit forces the apparently rigid structure of the list to flex and reform in order to encompass it, to absorb and account for a perturberant space that is always already inside the system.[9] However, such reorganizations of disorderly material are inherent in the processes of list systems. The conceptual construct we recognize as the list inevitably represents (formally and symbolically) a moment of stasis in an interminable series of decision points, a temporary order salvaged from the universal chaos and fixed in an informational singularity, an order that vanishes into the interstices of its own internal contradictions as soon as it is stabilized. Inscribing difference within a structure that privileges the same, the list simultaneously erases and sketches the sign of chaos.

Prior to list construction, chaos marks the site of the potential, the random, and the unselected. Free from constraint, essentially democratic, a chaotic pool of data somehow suggests a space of prelapsarian grace, a paradise of incoherence where no datum need account for its position and no class need ever be defined. However, without the intervention of some ordering process, that incoherent pool threatens to swamp information-transfer tasks, to spill over and through any neighboring structure where boundaries and limits have already been assigned.

The external structure of a list is a sort of information dam, separating two relatively fluid bodies of data—one chaotic, one ordered—from each other. That structure actualizes in graphic form a series of binary decisions opposing the necessary to the contingent and the eligible to the ineligible.[10] These binary decisions pull items out of the data pool and locate them inside a conceptual retaining wall whose rigid boundaries suggest that there is no space for the intermediate, that the dividing line between the included and the excluded cuts across all ambiguities and equivocations. Because this operation focuses on separation, the decisions must inevitably be based on difference, or upon fine distinctions between similarities;[11] otherwise, everything has equal eligibility for inclusion in the list, and chaos reigns on both sides of the barrier.

This structural insistence upon difference and the creation of boundaries may actually transform or deform the subject class.[12] Binary construction codes push the ordering intelligence toward overgeneralization, toward a radical reduction of actual relations to the necessarily digital relation that includes or excludes the item from the list or positions it within the list itself.[13] Since a potential class member generally has analogical relations or multiple relations with other potential members in the data pool, a digitalization of those relations conceals or suppresses a great deal of information about individual members and clearly sacrifices the integrity of the member for the coherence of the class. Stripped of ineligible or uncategorical characteristics, the actualized class member loses both context and a portion of its content when it crosses the boundary into the categorical realm.

Ironically, completed classes or lists still manage to suggest the presence of excluded data, to imply all the lists that might have been constructed out of the data pool; after all, the

> decision as to what to put in each place also
> depends on the possibility of putting a different
> element there instead, so that each choice which
> is made [involves] a complete reorganization
> of the structure, which [is never] the same as
> one vaguely imagined nor as some other which
> might have been preferred to it. (Lévi-Strauss
> 1966, 19)

Thus, there are shadows of unconstructed lists in the margins of list structures, faint suggestions of potentialities that, for one reason or another, were never realized. This doubled vision destabilizes the list, working against the analytical gaze that penetrates content and forces an atomistic account of reality.

Robert Harbison notes that list construction shatters ordinary perspective, making "a reader feel he did not know there were that many things in the world, that there is more to existence than he remembered" (1977, 159). Although this perspectival disorientation may be overwhelming, it also carries epistemological conviction. A naming of class members suggests a full presence and a complete account, implying that a precise articulation of component parts renders an accurate representation of the thing itself. Listing thus shifts visual (and linguistic) tracking operations away from the gestalt toward the component or the atom, away from systemic function toward the identification and placement of internal nodes. Ultimately, this microsystemic focus induces a sensation of full presence when only a series of particles has been encountered.

The particles themselves are decontextualized in the process, an operation that figures category boundaries as neutral containing devices whose main function is that of division. The component nodes of the list, once inside the boundary, primarily interact with each other; interactions across the boundary take place on a different scale as the gestalt entity instantiated by list construction responds to its environment and plays roles appropriate to its hyposystemic level. Separation of particles or component nodes from their relational and significatory context troubles some critics; Brian McHale points out that the decontextualization of listed items has the effect of "evacuating language of presence, leaving only a shell behind . . ." (1987, 153).[14] This suggests that list construction leaves blank spaces not only in the data pool but inside the list boundary itself—internal vacancies that can only be filled by the name of the list or class. In effect, then, the construction process subverts the ordering intention and redirects the gaze toward the process itself, leaving content in an unstable and untenable position.

Lévi-Strauss, in *The Savage Mind* (1966), examines categorical content and configuration in the light of a conceptual dichotomy between savage thought, a conceptual domain in which totalization of the concrete insists upon a devotion to order, and domesticated thought, a practical mental space from which the *bricoleur* operates upon and through whatever order is to hand as he engages in specific and limited projects. Jack Goody, in *The Domestication of the Savage Mind* (1977), disputes this primary opposition of savage and domesticated thought and offers instead a reading of the oral conceptual praxis against the written. To Goody, oral culture demands that mental constructions conform to severe temporal conditions; if information must be reproduced via either mimesis or memorial reconstruction, conceptual practice must provide forms that are either conveniently brief, strictly representative, rigidly coded for mnemonic recall, or designed for immediate disposal. Written culture, on the other hand, is extratemporal, and this permits abstraction of information and subsequent transfer of coded information forms; these can be used for many purposes, including storage, analysis, and gaming.

Goody assumes that oral cultures will not depend heavily on lists for information coding (although reconstructions of oral conceptual practices may indeed format those practices in list form when the oral culture comes under analysis). He argues that lists do not flourish as mental constructions until written culture offers them a stability and utility which oral culture cannot provide.

The written list, characterized by a physical location, multidirectional legibility, and precise boundaries, lends itself to categorical and other ordering processes.[15] Bound only by artificial storage capacity and not by memorial capacity, the written list takes many forms, absorbing variant amounts of information into flexible, plastic configurations. Written cultures are quick to take advantage of this versatile conceptual framework: Goody's research indicates that lists appear *with* writing, first in representational or content-bound forms and then in metaphorical and ludic forms.[16]

The basic shell structure or external cognitive form of the list tends to shape itself around three concepts—the inventory, the itinerary, and the lexicon (Goody 1977, 80).[17] The inventory has a transformative function,[18] replacing things with names and collecting them inside a conceptual frame that can interact on a cognitive, abstract level with other conceptual structures. Gass points out that this transformation inevitably alters the relations between the things listed, since items become co-present and contiguous inside the list in a way that may or may not reflect actual relations in the world (1985, 122). Inside the Gatsby list, for instance, the contiguity of members from East Egg suggests a unity or subcategorical membership that is entirely spurious in terms of member likeness although it is completely valid geographically. Similarly, their co-presence within Carraway's frame implies an unjustified temporal equivalence; in fact, the guests' appearances at Gatsby's spread over an entire summer, a variance that is not reflected by the construction of the list. Finally, the inventory frame asserts internal coherence and class consistency while offering an essentially nominal comprehension of a category that might have greater signification under different structural conditions.[19]

The itinerary is process-based, forming around a series of actual or suggested actions, just as Pynchon's Krupp menu does. Unlike other list forms, which conceal a necessarily synchronic temporality, the itinerary is overtly diachronic, and the relations of its members insist upon an extension of time across the list itself. The sequential quality of the itinerary provides an intimate link with narrative; thus, according to Barney, lists of actions "form a borderline between the syntagmatic and the paradigmatic—they are half story, half list" (1982, 202).

Lexicons are metagraphic, forming at a level above the inventory even though they assert a similar relationship between words and things. The lexicon, however, is an inventory of names or of significations. Like the list of synonyms for "whore," the lexicon is a collection of *means* of representation rather than a representation of some contextualized class.

Any list has an informational dimension, whether the list is oral or written. An external conceptual shell categorizes and digitalizes content, giving the collective presence a name that is transmissible even when content has been evacuated. However, the "dialectical effect of writing upon classification" is that it

> sharpens the outlines of the categories [and] encourages the hierarchisation of the classification system [while it] leads to questions about the nature of the classes through the very fact of placing them together. (Goody 1977, 102)

This interrogation of the class (made possible by the visibility of the written list) foregrounds and decontextualizes the category at the same time, removing the category from its conceptual ground in the same way the category distances the member from its data pool. A fundamental uncertainty about the validity of categorical statements arises from such an interrogation, which in turn problematizes the relationship of the category to context *and* to content—a dangerously chaotic destabilization of structure.

Nonpragmatic or ludic lists focus on structuration, pressing content components into exotic positions or twisting relational connectors so that intrasystemic configuration is strained and exposed to view. Such lists experiment with variant construction codes, foregrounding a wayward categorization process in which

the listed elements may not properly specify the
general principle adduced; the principle of the
list may seem to shift as the list is extruded;
the conclusion drawn from the list (if any) may
be irrelevant to the context; the very production
of the list in the circumstances may seem pedan-
tic, incongruously reflective, rhetorically
self-conscious, absurdly pompous, crudely self-
serving, or otherwise inappropriate to the speaker
or the situation; the list may go on too long for
its worth; [or] it may wildly jumble discordant
materials. (Barney 1982, 195–96)

Categorical play crystallizes problems of classification, re-
fracting the analytic gaze and generating new information about
previously static forms or classes. This new information may
then permit extension or redefinition of the category or suggest
alternative component figurations within the categorical frame.

Some critics fear that categorical diversion and analytical
abstraction may erect a conceptual prison, reinforcing the
separation of analyst from analysand and enclosing the organizing intelligence in an infinite regression of relationally
symmetrical structures. Viewed from this perspective, categorical play devolves from an arbitrary imposition of order upon
the data and abandons the premise that analysis may discover
or reflect existent order; Frank Kermode sees such activity,
along with "research into the autonomy of forms," as an
intramural response to a carceral experience of the world. In the
end, he suggests, we become totally absorbed in the "architecture of our own cells" (1967, 164–65).

Our cognitive enclosures nest inside similarly structured
cultural cells. Lists, as informational entities and systemic statements about epistemology, extend an investigation of construction codes outward toward culture, forging a link to discourses
of culture analysis and criticism. By its very nature, the list
provides a cultural perspective that is at once grand and mi-
croscopic, since it implies everything while mentioning only

selected items.[20] It facilitates a dialogue between the excluded multiverse and the included microverse that echoes a cultural debate about how information *may* be ordered and what information *is* to be ordered; essentially, the list exhibits the cultural episteme writ small.

Lévi-Strauss says that the "savage mind totalizes [and refuses] to allow anything human (or even living) to remain alien to it . . ." (1966, 245).[21] Similarly, Foucault describes "old history" as a "well-defined spatio-temporal area . . . with a system of homogenous relations . . . a network of causality [and] relations of analogy . . ." (1972, 9). Like the savage mind, old history wants to totalize elements; new history, on the other hand, tends to look at "series, divisions, limits, differences of level, shifts, chronological specificities, particular forms of rehandling, [and] possible types of relation" (1972, 10). The intellectual approach Lévi-Strauss names *bricolage* and Foucault "new history" parallels a systemic or organic understanding of relationality and seems to offer a radically different view of culture than paradigms bound by rigid systematization or codification.

Since the *bricoleur* depends upon fragments of preexisting order as material for his own intellectual projects, his approach has necessary ties to the analytical and categorical work of the savage scientist; similarly, narratives concerned with systemic organization of relatively autonomous components are underwritten by culturally constructed epistemological frames. The encyclopedic text, for instance, attempts to capture and critique cultural discourse systems by offering up a collection of fragments or lists culled from a temporally, geographically, or epistemologically specific data pool. The selection and construction process is then informed by the "ideological perspectives from which that culture shapes and interprets its knowledge" (Mendelson 1986, 30).

The encyclopedic project hovers between totalization and fragmentation, pitting the analytical gaze against the synthetic fusion or absorption functions of the narrative supersystem

(Mendelson 1986, 32).[22] As a functioning entity, it threatens
conceptual breakdown at every moment; since list structures
tend to question and contradict their own construction processes,
the systems that contain them must be prepared for internal
insurrection, categorical interrogation, and systemic reconfiguration as part of the ongoing effort at self-preservation.
Complete fluidity of structure would prevent instantiation of the
system and subvert the overall function of self-statement inherent in narratives; excessive rigidity would cause irreparable
fissures in internal structure under the pressure of chaotic intrusions. Thus the narrative is virtually forced to reside on
the unstable ground between analysis and synthesis; it must
have systemic boundaries that can absorb chaos while keeping
Chaos at bay.

Bachelard suggests that in "the wardrobe there exists a
center of order that protects the entire house against uncurbed
disorder" (1969, 79). In other words, within a defined structure,
chaos can be contained and decontaminated; similarly, lists contain chaos and by doing so protect the system around them from
the effects of textual turbulence. An accommodation with chaos
takes place in that "intimate space," and because the disorder
has been contained without being repressed, analytical *and*
dialectical functions can still proceed. Jacques Derrida, in his
essay on Emmanuel Levinas, points out that if we refuse to
"choose between the opening and the totality . . . [and decide
to] be incoherent, but without systematically resigning ourselves
to incoherence, [then the] possibility of the impossible system
will be on the horizon to protect us from empiricism" (1978,
84). Like Borges, who stakes out a conceptual territory where
an uncategorical category may exist within a conventional
ordering system, Derrida suggests that controlled incoherence
is a survival mechanism, an intellectual window in an otherwise
impermeable cell.

Stuffed Parrots

The encyclopedia and the museum are paral-
lel projects: both attempt to reconstitute an essentially absent
subject by means of a synchronically situated and spatially
coherent collection of substantive fragments. One suggests that
a system of knowledge can be fragmented, rearranged, and
recreated as a textually and conceptually coherent representation of an information category; the other, that categorical statements can be articulated by disparate sets of objects joined
under an enforced and arbitrary order.

Clearly both projects must therefore concern themselves
with the identification and arrangement of constituent parts, a
process that locates constituent energy in individual components
and eventually effaces the significance of relational connectors
and construction functions. Indeed, the most consistent and
effective statements emanating from these projects may be
epistemological ones. In spite of a systematic focus on fragments, these projects do finally conserve and transfer sets of
construction codes, inscribing within their structures cultural
assumptions about acceptable reconfigurations of resistant and
necessarily incomplete constellations of data.[1]

In similar fashion, personal historiography locates an absent subject in a collation of temporally and spatially decontextualized personal data, an action that shifts the project toward a representation of the process rather than a comprehension of the subject. Whether figured as novel, biography, or autobiography, personal documentation foregrounds the structuration of the data into a model that asserts a totalization of the subject, a systematized and allegedly coherent statement of authority. Ironically, the necessary focus of the analytical (and authoritative) gaze upon the datic components of the subject subverts this attempt at coherence; analysis activates a fetishization process that tends to separate data from relational configuration and collapse the totalizing structure into itself. In the end, the document embodies an arbitrary articulation of overdetermined and radical components into a systemically functioning entity that states itself *as* a documentary system rather than a representation of the targeted subject.

This is precisely the difficulty facing Geoffrey Braithwaite, the narrator of Julian Barnes's *Flaubert's Parrot* (1984). His projected document, which asserts a representation of Gustave Flaubert within disparate sets of systematized data, shatters under the effects of the analytic gaze. Fixed by the gaze and fixing its focus, Braithwaite's concentrated datic components absorb constructive energy, weakening the already tenuous connections between his arbitrarily contiguous structures. The projected integrated representation vanishes in the process, since it must always be assumed but can never be seen whole by a gaze locked into analytical endeavors. And Flaubert disappears under analysis, leaving the articulated fragments with no principle of coherence beyond the internal frames embedded in Braithwaite's document.

Braithwaite's encyclopedic or biographic task is initiated by a conflict embodied in the collections of two Flaubert museums; two stuffed parrots, each of which claims authenticity as the "Loulou" which inspired Flaubert's "*Un coeur simple,*" occupy a datic space with room for only one. This informational paradox is one which must be resolved if a totalized understanding of Flaubert is to be achieved; he cannot, after all, have been inspired by *both,* since his documentary records reflect the presence of only one. Braithwaite's investigative and interpretive activities thus begin with an attempt to authenticate a unique parrot, an attempt to clear the system of the noise generated by this equivocal claim.

Braithwaite imposes a circular analytic structure upon this endeavor. He has already singled out the parrot as a uniquely explanatory object; to him it occupies a systemically central position through which many of the information paths encoding Flaubert pass or finally connect. He believes an apprehension of the parrot will decipher an entire set of codes, unlocking the secrets of the Flaubert system. This belief leads to a project that plans a totalization of Flaubert built upon and around the stuffed parrot and a stabilization of the parrot within a cage constructed out of an integrated Flaubertian code.

In the process, Braithwaite assembles, collates, and, eventually, fabricates data that, in the variety of their patterns and configurations, suggest a potentially comprehensive discovery or representation of Flaubert. However, the informational models encoding Flaubert in Braithwaite's final document valorize fragmentation as a means of representation, actualizing in their structures the arbitrary and incomplete nature of personal historiography.[2] Braithwaite depends heavily upon list structures, forms haunted by the shadows of excluded data: chronologies, compendia of quotations, a bestiary, a compilation of testimony, a railway guidebook, a dictionary, an examination paper—forms inevitably foregrounding the struggle to maintain a secure categorical border and stabilize an enclosed data pool constantly threatened by structural collapse or chaotic intrusion. Further, these all provide data in configurations that cannot possibly be symmetrical with the set of relations that formerly existed between the data and Flaubert himself. The relations exhibited in Braithwaite's structures are necessarily dominated by his own interpretive frame and therefore do not replicate a preexisting order. Finally, the document Braithwaite constructs, being marked by a radically constrained selection process as well as a skewed articulationprocess, is neither simulation nor conceptual map. Rather, its mosaic effect pushes it toward the status of documentary museum, a relationally randomized collection of disparate items placed together under an assumption that spatial contiguity enacts conceptual contiguity, and that subject comprehension can rise up out of datic conglomeration.[3]

Conventional biography insists that subject comprehension rises out of encyclopedic narration, that a sequential rendering of an entire data pool—or as much of it as the biographer can collect—comes nearest to replication of a subject. Braithwaite avoids this form of representation, limiting himself to narratives about his own life and to a fabulous construction of "Louise Colet's" version.[4] These two narratives swerve the analytical focus away from Flaubert and toward the representation of allegedly peripheral figures. Covertly, of course, any such project demands a continually split focus, for narrators unavoidably abandon (and lose control over) their subjects while they narrate and instantiate themselves in the process of narration; thus, Braithwaite's document slides toward self-totalization even as it works to encircle Flaubert, and his narrative persona necessarily fabulates Flaubert as much as the Colet "version" does.

A fragmentary and incomplete Braithwaite autobiography nests within his fragmented biography of Flaubert. Here, as the writer and reader of his own life, Braithwaite

> inhabits the hermeneutic universe where all
> understanding takes place. [He] serves, by this
> habitation, as the paradigmatic reader; and the
> autobiographical text, embodying this reading,
> becomes, in turn, a model of the possibilities and
> problems of all interpretive activity. (Gunn
> 1982, 22)

Strained by a role that requires him to be both inside and outside his text, Braithwaite conflates his multiple textual relations with the relational node occupied by Charles Bovary, figuring his own wife as Emma and Flaubert as another erotic partner who remains elusive and unfaithful to the end.[5] The fragmented document that ultimately encloses both biography and auto-biography foregrounds the limitations of interpretation as much as it does the impossibility of reconstructing a lost or contextually dislocated data pool; the autobiographer is no more able to escape the effects of intratextual (or intrasystemic) noise on his own reception and interpretation of personal history than he is able to encode an informational model that will transfer a seamless and noiseless text to a targeted reader.[6]

Braithwaite is clearly drawn to closed structures. Each of the informational models he chooses has a generic claim to closure, to at least a temporary totality as comprehensive representation of its topical field. And, having already associated himself with *Bovary,* he manages to imply a link to *Bouvard and Pécuchet* as well when he adopts this particular range of information structures. In fact, he follows quite closely a biographic methodology established by the two unfortunate copy clerks. In the midst of a bout with history, Bouvard and Pécuchet decide to write "the life of the Duc d'Angoulême." After two weeks of research in the municipal library, they enclose their subject in a series of fragmentally constituted structures: a chronology, a guide to significant bridges, a testament of virtues, a selection of "intimate details" from childhood, and a collation of "apt remarks" and written "proclamations" (Flaubert 1976, 124–25). Finally, before they are called away by a realization that "external facts . . . must be completed by psychology" (Flaubert 1976, 129), and thus to new researches and an eventual abandonment of their biographical project, Bouvard and Pécuchet note down that they must "look into the Prince's amours"—thus completing the structural symmetry between their methodology and Braithwaite's subsequent attempt to reconstitute Flaubert.[7]

Bouvard and Pécuchet exhibit an essentially textual, encyclopedic approach to knowledge. As if turning the pages in a huge encyclopedia, they begin with agriculture and riffle through the physical and social sciences, immersing themselves in each one and exhausting it completely before moving on to the next. However, like the topical entries in an encyclopedia, and like Braithwaite's individual information models, the subject areas they study remain separate. Bouvard and Pécuchet treat knowledge as a succession of closed systems, a series so isolated that information from one area never slips over to inform another. Charles Bernheimer notes that the

> clerks make no instructive connections between their various failures. Each remains isolated, and their very lives seem to reflect this fragmented and discontinuous structure. It is as if their subjectivities were recreated with each new code they fetishize and existed only as long as the unifying function of that code remained in force. (1984, 168)

Because they cannot integrate the fragmented results of their studies, the two clerks become like closed systems themselves, with the temporary order induced by a period of study consuming itself in its own construction and immediately breaking down into disorder once the next task begins.

Bernheimer links the clerks' fetishization of separate subject areas to an avoidance of the encompassing or integrated vision. Such a vision, he believes, would necessarily reveal the clerks' sexual equivalence, a similarity concealed beneath the differentially expressed gender roles they have chosen to play inside their own relational system. Thus, the "function they expect [each book] to perform is fetishistic in that its role is to signify and systematize difference precisely by denying the *reality* of difference" (1984, 165). Each topic becomes invested with erotic energy as it consumes or absorbs the significance that would otherwise inhere in the informative statements of an integrated and functional system. A gaze focused upon the component to the exclusion of the whole, a gaze concentrated on the differences articulated within the body of knowledge, thereby escapes a disturbing recognition of an extrasystemic sexual similarity and social difference.

According to Bernheimer, "the erotic fantasy that sustains the clerks' enterprises is the conception of a fully interpreted and intelligible world that would dissolve all difference between nature and culture by assimilating both into a uniform code of signification" (1984, 166). Bouvard and Pécuchet are committed to the encyclopedic perspective, to totalizations that can situate each datic component in an appropriate and fully explicable (and explicatory) position. They wish for a world that is fully encoded and textualized, and thus completely accessible to the student. The creation of such a code, however, involves an inevitable fetishization of the encoded data. Baudrillard says that in fetishism,

> it is the passion of the code that expresses itself. Regulating and subordinating at once objects and subjects, this passion gives them both over to abstract manipulation. . . . The actual fetishism of the object attaches itself to the object-sign emptied of its substance and of its history, reduced to being the mark of a difference and the resume of a whole system of differences. (quoted in Bernheimer 1984, 162)[8]

The passion of the code ironically defeats attempts at totalization. Abstraction removes the datic component from context, placing a categorical shell where an object once resided; it then injects an eroticized gaze into that empty space, making the component node a site of fixation and seduction—suggesting a terminal function the component node is systemically unable to perform. Since components are dedicated to an integral entity, no one node is capable of complete systemic statement; the fixated node can neither release nor return the gaze.

A systematic totalization requires a precise and stabilized articulation of parts, the sort of precision and stasis that does not inhere in systems actually existing in the world.

Nevertheless, the analytic gaze attempts that articulation, focusing upon the operations and relations of individual components until the presumably stable structure shifts and alters in response to this influx of energy and the perturberant effects of fixation. Under the analytic gaze, until chaos-management techniques can be initiated, isolated components acquire excess significance and an erasure of systemic identity begins.

Braithwaite's biographic project suffers precisely this fate. His desire for a fully present Flaubert encourages an erotic but futile fetishization of the data. His informational models suggest a containment of the subject, but data left outside the model are equally Flaubertian and potentially substantive of the desired presence. In the end, "Flaubert doesn't return the gaze" (1). Rather, dispersed and fragmented by Braithwaite's fetishization, he draws the eye into a labyrinthine documentary museum. There, endless reconfigurations of component relations occupy and finally debilitate the focusing mechanism that constitutes the analytical gaze.

Braithwaite's documentary museum mirrors the one created by Bouvard and Pécuchet as they collect objects related to their various subjects. Unlike an encyclopedia, which pretends to comprehension and to an articulation of specific relations, the museum strives toward inference. It collects tokens associated with the absent subject and implies by their presence a transcendental representation, a coherence indicated but not reproduced by the relations exhibited within it. Bouvard and Pécuchet's museum, unlike an encyclopedic totalization, preserves the heterogeneity of components even though a subsequent analysis of their intrasystemic positions may assign them to classes which suggest a preexisting systematization of the material. For instance, Douglas Crimp notes that many of the items in the clerks' museum can be categorized as symbols of the phallus; still, the objects within the museum retain their artifactual heterogeneity, an essential dissimilarity which "defies the systematization and homogenization that [the clerks' search for] knowledge [demands]" (1983, 49).

The subversive presence of this museum within the clerks' home suggests a tacit acknowledgment that their project has all along tended toward collection rather than systematization. The museum records a progress through topical fields that have resisted comprehension; instead, the fields have yielded up associative tokens that mark the initial presence and subsequent departure of the subject. These tokens, the artifacts in the museum, defy classification because they are drawn from disparate categories and assembled without design. Any coherence within the museum itself is accidental, situational, and emblematic of the self-organizing potential of randomized bits of data.[9]

Eugenio Donato contends that the clerks' eventual move toward an arbitrary imposition of relation upon serendipitously collected objects is prefigured in an early series of Parisian institutions: the clerks visit "old curiosity shops . . . the Conservatory of Arts and Crafts, Saint-Denis, the Gobelins, the Invalides and all the public collections . . . the Museum . . . the Louvre . . . [and] the Central Library . . ." (Flaubert 1976, 28). Donato points out that the "bric-a-brac" encountered in the curiosity shops and reincarnated in the clerks' home museum is not textualized, is not "in the library," but rather initiates a conceptual series that *contains* the library; he finds it significant that this series "contains one term that itself contains a heterogeneous series, namely the *Museum . . .*" (1986, 210). This concatenation of a series headed by the curiosity shop and containing the equally heterogeneous museum sets up a regression of similarly heterogeneous structures, a slippage through descending levels that is finally halted when Bouvard and Pécuchet enter and become artifacts in their own arbitrary and heterogeneous universe.

Braithwaite's documentary museum is likewise prefigured by an early visit to institutions containing serendipitous collections of Flaubertiana. These two museums, one located within the Hôtel-Dieu in Rouen (where Flaubert's father had been employed as a surgeon), one at the Flaubert summer house in Croisse, are constructed out of remainders, remnants of Flaubert that have become available or that were haphazardly preserved.

As such, they are eclectic, offering the visitor a selection of Flaubert tokens related to each other *as* tokens of Flaubert rather than by a narrational scheme of explication.[10] Like a tangible list of otherwise unrelated items gathered together under a generative categorical head, the museum artifacts are only tenuously related and are thus highly subject to chaotic intrusions. The presence of the two competing parrots, for instance, disrupts the integrity of both museums, interrogating the selection and construction processes underlying each museum's design.[11]

The museum, however, is equipped to deal with such intrusions. Since it does not depend upon rigid coherence and systematization for structural identity, the museum absorbs or deletes awkward class members without thereby declaring a violation of categorical premises. Although its project is initially archeological—it discovers, preserves, and arranges tokens—the construction codes that enable the museum also subvert the designs of any totalizing intelligence attempting an interpretation of the tokens, frustrating the gaze that wants to find a deeply explanatory significance within this essentially contingent structure.[12]

The biographic museum Braithwaite constructs is similarly subversive. His fragments are arbitrarily collected and arranged, foregrounding a set of research procedures and construction codes rather than a system of Flaubertian facts and relations. Further, his information models encode datic resistance to fixed interpretation; he offers, for instance, two equally plausible chronologies of significant events in Flaubert's life, one documenting a successful and fulfilling career, one a desperate and unhappy search for acceptance and recognition.

Even as they claim authority as tokens of Flaubert, the museum documents question the biographic and archeological processes involved in their creation. For example, Braithwaite's interest in the parrot encourages him to construct a bestiary. This document parodies biographic exegesis and doubts the ability of any such structure to provide significant information.[13] The bestiary has an unbalanced internal structure that records and foregrounds a tendency toward differential treatment of subject matter: the bear and the parrot are discussed at great and excessively critical length, while the camel and sheep get relatively short shrift. In addition, this information model contains within it sublevels of structure that magnify and ridicule the classification process; four subcategories of dogs (romantic, practical, figurative, and drowned/fantastical) are listed, and the "practical" category includes a detailed chronology of Flaubertian encounters with individual dogs.

Although the museum itself can absorb and utilize chaos in the creation of new datic arrangements, the narrator's inability to prevent the intrusion of Braithwaitiana into his documentary tokens of Flaubert points out the essential permeability of information structures. The "train-spotters guide to Flaubert," for instance, conflates Braithwaite and Flaubert as it renders a selection of railway excursions endured by both biographer and subject. And in a similar blending of the two lives competing for instantiation in this document, Braithwaite creates his own "Dictionary of Accepted Ideas" which, upon publication, mirrors and undermines the authority of Flaubert's dictionary just as the two parrots mock and compete with each other.

The subversive activities of the individual documents force continual rearrangement of museum tokens and suggest highly contingent interpretations of datic and modular relations to the targeted subject. Finally, Braithwaite's document collapses into itself, acknowledging an intrinsic inability to capture biography or even the authentic parrot. At the end of the novel, Braithwaite discovers the source of both parrots: inside the Natural History Museum, a roomful of stuffed and sardonic parrots glares down at him as he realizes that any one of them (or none) might be the parrot "Loulou."

Braithwaite's discovery suggests that the museum, like the encyclopedia, is finally contingent and susceptible to chaotic intrusions that threaten the stability of systematic representation. Like Bouvard and Pécuchet, he finds that all closed systems run down toward irredeemable chaos. Indeed, Donato points out that what

thermodynamics makes impossible is a history
conceived as archeology. In the long run, the
metaphors of thermodynamics will rob Cuvier's
geology, as well as the museums of natural or
human artifacts, of any epistemological privilege, reducing them to the status of a bric-a-brac
collection of disparate objects . . . (1986, 218)

In other words, thermodynamics works against any design
privileging closed or static order; in such a system, the components lose significance as soon as they begin to break free of
their established positions.[14] That process is accelerated by the
analytic gaze, which fetishizes components and removes them
from their systemic context; however, even without the action
of the gaze, the closed system is doomed to break down under
the dissipative force of time.

Bouvard and Pécuchet exhibits "in part an epistemological
nihilism that denounces the possibility of ever attaining an
essential knowledge of the world, [and] manifests itself more
explicitly as a historical nihilism" (Donato 1986, 219); this is
so because thermodynamics (which is specifically mentioned
in the text) suggests an erasure of difference and a consequent
loss of origin, pointing toward a final end to time and order. The
world of the two copy clerks is finally one of absence, for neither their epistemology nor their historical moments suggest the
possibility of a recovery of presence.

Flaubert's Parrot seems to imply a similar nihilism, and
Braithwaite's fragmentation of order may be an effort to capture and mark the absence that lies beneath (or perhaps deep
within) systematical projects. In his work on Diderot, Jochen
Schulte-Sasse points out that the modern sensibility demands
this sort of marking; he notes that the absence textualized in the
tableau, the observed fragment privileged in Diderot's narratives, is

the structural equivalent of an infinite cycle of
desire and fulfillment engendered by the differ-

entiation of society into complementary subsystems. For in a society structured by a logic of
complementation, fulfillment has to be broken up
into components that only can be experienced
successively. (1985, 107)[15]

The fragments Braithwaite offers as biography likewise
suggest a compartmentalized subjectivity and an experience
of the systemic that reduces comprehension to a necessarily
partial apprehension under the pressure of desire and chaotic
breakdown.

On the other hand, Braithwaite is trapped within his
own systematic project and cannot therefore obtain a metasystemic view of the relations he has established in his attempt
to enclose Flaubert. Although constructed out of fragments, the
work functions as an integrated whole: the complete text operates systemically as an instantiation of Braithwaite's investigative and interpretive project—a realization not of a Flaubert
biography, but of a coherent and comprehensible narrative
project whose subject is finally itself.

At this level, what had been perceived as a destructive operation of intra- and extrasystemic chaos upon Braithwaite's
systematization of Flaubert is now revealed as healthy turbulence occurring within a self-organizing narrative structure, as
instability inside a system which feeds upon the ambiguities
produced in its components and which is completely engaged
in the reconfiguration of its own relations. Rather than a nihil-
istic statement, then, the message of *Flaubert's Parrot* may be
a regenerative one, a statement about the fragmentation, and
restructuration, of information. As an essentially contingent narrative system, *Flaubert's Parrot* refuses to enact totality and
thus need fear neither the scattering effects of the gaze nor
the effects of chaotic intrusion. Thus understood, the novel expresses itself as a project which heeds Monsieur Jeufroy's
warning to Bouvard and Pécuchet: "Don't torment yourself.
Anyone who tries to get to the bottom of everything is sliding
down a dangerous slope" (Flaubert 1976, 234).

chapter 9

The Cultural Hypersystem

*From a field perspective, interfaces
are not barriers, but points of exchange,
surfaces through which two orders of
being can interpenetrate. This raises
the possibility of a holistic field that
transcends and includes the interface.*

—*N. Katherine Hayles*
The Cosmic Web

Thin and permeable conceptual membranes
separate systems from each other. These interfaces permit the
exchange of information and a mutual systemic influence, acting
as facilitators as much as inhibitors. One might think of the
system of interfaces as a neural network, a web of metaphorically fibrous connectors across which information codes ripple
and resonate throughout a larger, more complex information
entity. The interfaces between narrative supersystems, for instance, form the relational skeleton of a hypersystem which we
might otherwise name literary discourse. This hypersystem, like
other structures in the systemic hierarchy, instantiates itself in
its relations, which express component positioning and information flow patterns. Its self-statement provides a structural
code for the creation of statements of and about literature.

Operating at a high level of systemic autonomy, hypersystems are isomorphic with the discourse structures conceived
by Foucault. These, he says, can be identified through a process
that characterizes and individualizes

> the coexistence of . . . dispersed and hetero-
> geneous statements; the system that governs
> their division, the degree to which they depend
> upon one another, the way in which they inter-
> lock or exclude one another, the transformation
> that they undergo, and the play of their location,
> arrangement, and replacement. (1972, 34)[1]

Identifiable by correspondent means, the literary hypersystem
depends upon configurative processes similar to those enacted
in its component parts—and interacts with other discourse systems to construct an information network inside a cultural
system, continuing a conceptual isomorphism that reaches up
and down the hierarchy of information entities.[2]

Functioning as an infodynamically open system, culture
states itself through a self-organizing chaos-management structure, monitoring and reconfiguring its internal hypersystems in
an effort to maintain stability while permitting growth and innovation.[3] Internal activity is constant and competitive within
this system, as components extract information from each other
and work to suppress noise and absorb chaos. In the process,
component nodes frequently shift tasks and tenants in response
to intrasystemic needs. As monitoring duties, for instance, pass
from one discourse system to another (say, from a theological
hypersystem to a secular one), this forces a rearrangement
of the relations between the two discourses or requires the
acquisition of new tenants for discourse positions.[4] Exchanges
across the systemic boundary also take place: other cultures
exert pressure on the system, impinging upon self-statement
functions by forwarding information or chaotic elements
through the interface, and the cultural system itself may export
information or chaos in an effort to release internal pressure

or remove perturberant data. In either case, conditions may induce reconfigurative activity.

This view of culture posits a universe committed to orderly behavior, a universe in which even chaos eventually resolves into order. Representing that behavior as taking place within hierarchies of relational systems that stack and interlock—within hierarchies[5] that are conceptually, if not structurally, stable—a systemic theory of culture is essentially ecological and global.[6] Such an approach suggests broad applications of knowledge (and intuition) about the way information is organized and transmitted, and provides metaphors for understanding complex organisms which might otherwise evade analysis. Consequently, it exhibits a totalizing impulse that is radically at odds with its postmodern focus on local information and dynamic processes. Indeed, Hayles fore-grounds this duality in her recent work on chaos theory. She points out that chaos science offers a doubled response to its subject, one that privileges the undecidability of chaotic systems even as it attempts to confine chaos within theoretical bound-aries. By insisting upon a fundamental order beneath even the most turbulent systemic behavior, she says, chaos science limits through nominative and descriptive mastery a potentially dangerous force, defusing the threat inherent in uncontrolled chaos (1990,173).[7] Likewise, a systemic theory of culture valo-rizes the innovative potential of discourse systems at the same time as it attempts to totalize and stabilize culture within a fun-damentally synthetic representation. From this paradoxical, Borgesian position, systems theory insists upon the validity of its own explanation even as it demands an acknowledgment that analysis is not only inadequate but also potentially destructive.

Depending heavily on modeling and metaphoric intuition, systems analysis operates at the edge of the Baudrillardian hyperreal.[8] This postmodern conception of an overanalyzed universe coincides, for Baudrillard, with the concerns an-nounced in contemporary narrative. There he discovers a technique which subsumes both sense and subject beneath an objectivity which is finally that of the "pure look—objectivity at last liberated from the object, that is nothing more than the blind relay station of the look which sweeps over it" (1983, 143).[9] In contemporary representation, he suggests, the object is called forth to submit to a "severe interrogation of its scattered fragments" and to the operations of the optic. These operations, which are similar to strategies embodied in postmodern narrative, dismantle or alter the object or exaggerate articulation until the joints fail to hold. Under one sequence, analysis by the optic collapses the object into a collection of its parts or reduplicates the object until it becomes merely serial and no longer representational. Alternatively, the optic engages the object in the seductive play of contiguity, a hesitation of the gaze between the object and its serial reproductions that substitutes for genuine attention. Still another operation turns the gaze away from repetition to modulation, seeking signification in "minimal separation" and in the small modulation that breaks the series and opens a new set of *different* objects.[10] All of these, Baudrillard suggests, involve a return to binarism and a reinforcement of the digital code (1983, 144–45).

The differential functions internalized in systems threaten an activation of or entry into the hyperreal. Within the bounds of any information entity, filtration and monitoring functions continually make digital decisions, reducing analog representations of data to categorical or transmissible forms—a decontextualization similar to the liberation of object Baudrillard warns against. In effect, systems exist inside a digital space even though they also inhabit (and constitute) a gestalt.[11] And inside this digital realm, systems subject data to an infinity of tests, a "continual procedure of directed interrogation" which encodes and controls data.[12] Consequently, systemic testing (which regularly occurs in the construction of a list, for instance) pushes the data base toward the hyperreal and evacuates systemic identity, suggesting to the observer that the system itself may simply be a tested and reproduced version of a statement rather than a contextually and actually informative name.

Paradoxically, however, chaos theory suggests that no name has ever been possible; under this dispensation, systems are granted a fundamental anonymity that parallels their autonomy. Because theoretical inquiry is directed toward unstable and turbulent open systems,[13] any optical examination initiated under chaos theory requires a contingent focus, an extremely wide frame, and/or a time-elapse mechanism (which permits full investigation only as retrospective). In a certain sense, then, rigorous interrogation or analytical reproduction of the chaotic gestalt simply cannot take place; diachronically defined and tracked, the open and autonomous system moves too rapidly and unpredictably for the focused gaze. Direct analysis may foreground components in synchronic and instantly obsolete still shots,[14] but the gestalt escapes or survives this reduction because of its innate capacity for immediate and variant reconfiguration.

In the end, the duality of systems analysis encourages interpretive hesitation: oscillating between inside and outside, enticed by internal functions that encourage and respond to the analytic gaze and simultaneously repelled by an external uncertainty that refuses all attempts at penetration, the student of systems inhabits a critical gap. From this position, theoretical totalizations expose their fissures, as polymorphous structures imply representational statements suitable to the Borgesian heterocosm. A natural and culturally appropriate similarity thus exists between scientific paradigms for chaotic systems and deconstructive critical practice.

Hayles argues that literary theories of deconstruction are equivalent to modern scientific theories which see chaos as productive of alternative systems; in both methodologies, she points out, new value structures have arisen in which "chaos is privileged over order, [and] increasing information over closure" (1987, 122).[15] Further, she considers that the conceptual isomorphism between the two is an expression of forces and relations in the cultural matrix rather than a case of influence across disciplines. In a symmetrically constitutive process,

> [deconstruction] and information theory then
> feed back into the culture to help create a
> cultural climate that sees the separation of sign
> from signification, message from meaning, as
> an important part of the postmodern condition.
> (1987, 124)

In other words, chaos theory and deconstructive theory are similar hypersystems within an enclosing and enabling culture; acting as environmental perturbations (and information transferral nodes) for each other, they also inform the culture, which subsequently feeds back reinforcing structures into these two potentially chaotic internal components.

Paulson suggests that literature constitutes an intrasystemic perturbation within culture, a source of noise that must be either suppressed or absorbed if the cultural system is to function successfully.[16] Literary noise, in this figuration, disturbs and then enlivens culture, acting first as a chaotic intrusion and finally as information encoding new structures or relations. Paulson points out that deconstruction is essentially a theory of textual noise because it suggests that "the message is not always received, intact, as it was sent, and the very concept or possibility of 'message' is simultaneously structured and undone by the possibility of its dispersion" (1988, 92). Deconstruction rectifies textual ambiguity by figuring uncertainty as a basis for discourse, thus encoding deferral and dispersion as valid information structures which can be transmitted across the discipline and exported into the culture.

Ultimately, the legitimacy of chaos or noise rests at the base of both deconstruction and systems theory. Lyotard points out that

> postmodern science—by concerning itself with
> such things as undecidables, the limits of precise
> control, conflicts characterized by incomplete
> information, *"fracta,"* catastrophes, and prag-
> matic paradoxes—is theorizing its own evolution

> as discontinuous, catastrophic, nonrectifiable,
> and paradoxical. . . . And it suggests a model of
> legitimation that has nothing to do with maxi-
> mized performance, but has as its basis differ-
> ence understood as paralogy. (1984, 60)[17]

This model of legitimation finds value in permutation (or reconfiguration) rather than performance, so that a discourse, or
system, might be measured against its capacity for innovation
or chaotic generation instead of its evocation of a particular state
or structure. Thus, paralogic differences are differences of relation which lead to further differentiation—providing endless
potential for systemic growth and preventing totalization of the
system at any point in its lifespan.

Lyotard argues that a science committed to paralogical legitimation makes it necessary to posit

> the existence of a power that destabilizes the
> capacity for explanation. . . . [It] is always lo-
> cally determined [and in] terms of the idea of
> transparency, it is a factor that generates blind
> spots and defers consensus. (1984, 61)

Such a science looks toward noise (incomplete explanation or
dissent) as a means of defusing the analytic gaze, occupying the
optic with local applications and forcing the continual dispersal
of observer energy. In Lyotard's estimation, this beneficial fragmentation or localization subverts the analytic attempt to totalize
the system and concentrates power in small, consensually defined sites. To some extent, then, localization disempowers the
hypersystem in favor of its own intrasystemic, chaotic components.[18] It also separates the components from their context,
effacing the very relations that establish identity, an effect
Lyotard neglects as he asks us to "wage a war on totality . . .
[and to] activate the differences and save the honor of the name"
(1984, 82).

Like Lyotard, Hayles clearly favors a systems or chaos-theoretical approach to literature and culture; however, she also expresses concern about the socio-political consequences of increasing differentiation. She points out that language, context, and time have all been "denatured" as each has been redefined by modern and postmodern relational theories. A reinscription of the human as a relationally constituted term or position seems, in her mind, a logical consequence of this trend (1990, 266). Thus revealed by theoretical discourse, the denatured human defines a position marked by loss of presence, an object distanced from the observer or a subject duplicated and split by self-scrutiny. Resisting cohesion with larger entities, submissive to local investigation and regulation, the denatured human finally represents itself as a purely consensual construct, separated from context and drained of content, ready to be modeled, replicated, and replaced.

When he moves to West Egg, Jay Gatsby vacates his past and enters a Baudrillardian hyperspace where everything stands at right angles to reality. Distanced from the originary Jimmy Gatz, removed from context and exhibiting no content, the man who inhabits the mansion is essentially a replicant, a facsimile of a Gatsby who can never be accurately stated.

The owl-eyed (nameless) man who admires Gatsby's library understands that a process of replication has taken place; when he sees that Gatsby's books are real (in a way that Gatsby himself is not) Owl-eyes exclaims to Carraway:

> It's a triumph. What thoroughness! What realism! Knew when to stop, too—didn't cut the pages. But what do you want? What do you expect? (46)

Focusing on Gatsby's skilled representation of himself as a man of taste and education, he comprehends the targeted position as one that requires only a limited realism and not the thing itself.

However, his tribute ironically marks Gatsby's failure; his perception confirms that Gatsby has not occupied the position of the projected "genuine" Gatsby, and that the statement of the mansion has therefore been garbled in transmission.

The exchange in the library identifies the mansion as a locus of alterity, as a space inhabited by unstable objects whose relation to context must be suspect. Gatsby, of course, is one of those objects: a token in his own museum, a self objectified both by his own introspection and the distanced gaze of his party guests. The exchange also mimics Carraway's own analytic project when it calls for a set of expectations against which the realistic library can be measured. Carraway, like the other guests, measures Gatsby against the public conception of the man as well as Gatsby's own claims to successful replication;[19] in the end, he participates in Gatsby's complete abandonment of subjectivity by recreating him in narrative.

Baudrillard notes that we are all the subject of ethnological reconstruction, for we live under the glare of examination in a world "completely catalogued and analysed and then artificially revived as though real, in a world of simulation . . ." (1983, 16). Carraway approaches Gatsby as if he were an alien culture, codifying his relationships, recording the reports of informants, tracing and translating his creation myths. In the process, Gatsby as subject disappears; instead, he becomes a body of knowledge, a transmissible information structure with a name twice removed from the original man.

Gatsby's position at the center of the guest list enacts a cultural statement about the way objects (even human objects) can be known. In Gatsby's world, things are already denatured, distanced by observer evaluations and extracontextual or imaginary relations. Carraway, for instance, envisions Gatsby in Louisville excited by the many men who had loved Daisy before him (148). Gatsby retains his quantitative nature in this vision, but even accurate recreation voids objective presence. Thus, the Carraway version displaces the West Egg Gatsby representation, modulating a replication and thereby threatening an infinite serial regression of hyperreal simulacra.

Gatsby himself is deeply involved in similar projects. Having renovated and recreated his own identity, he dreams of reproducing earlier relations with Daisy, telling Carraway that the past can certainly be repeated if he can only "fix everything just the way it was before" (111). He looks to simulation to locate and fix a Daisy who has been removed by time and experience from the position she occupied in Louisville and to recreate a set of relations that have naturally altered over time. His investment in simulation prevents an accommodation with the present and troubles an already unstable subjectivity.

An unstable subject position provides opportunities for objective intrusion and occupation. In the Gatsby hyperworld, groups of tokens enter into subject sites and even replace isolable objects. The green light on the dock is one among a number of "enchanted objects" (94) that substitute for Daisy, occupying her relational position until her presence finally dismantles the category. An overdetermined pile of shirts pushes Daisy into tears (93), erasing an important Gatsby statement under sensory signals directed at color, line, and texture. And, when Mr. McKee's set of city scenes rises like a nightmare into a drunken space between Myrtle's apartment and Carraway's cold bench at Pennsylvania Station (38), McKee's vision of the city disappears under a series of mumbled titles, leaving Carraway with another list that fails either to encapsulate or to cohere. In each case, a collection of tokens substitutes for a single object or statement and permits the elision of a potentially disturbing presence.

Indeed, ordering processes on Long Island are noticeably incoherent, severing information from purpose, space from position, and self from subjectivity. On the morning of Gatsby's death, Carraway kills time by making lists of stock quotations (155). This nondirected task models but does not constitute a purposive information construction process. The structure that results is an empty one, with no message that can be forwarded to any receiver. In her New York apartment, Myrtle Wilson makes lists of things to acquire or do (37), but these lists are only relevant within that isolated city space; she cannot transfer her plans to her alternative systemic position without revealing her duality and introducing chaos into the Valley of Ashes. And young Gatsby in Minnesota orders his day around a self-improvement schedule and a set of resolutions (174). As early evidence of a split subjectivity, this project shows a Gatsby already distanced from himself and straddling an internal gap which will subsequently extend itself across his external world. As the sign of a man eventually encircled and effaced by systematization, young Gatsby's list is dismally prophetic.

Human positions within this strange and inordinate system are based upon possession and destruction; relations fracture and shatter in response to turbulence, and reintegration comes from external impositions of order rather than interactive reconfiguration. Nick's narrative accuses Daisy and Tom of seeing others as objects to be smashed and left for still others to clean up (180–81). This suggests that Gatsby's disintegration can be attributed primarily to the Buchanans, that it results from outside (and identifiable) pressure. Carraway's accusation further indicates his belief that the fragmented Gatsby can be rectified by narrative—again, a completely external operation.

In the end, Gatsby cannot be reintegrated. He remains forever fragmented by Carraway's analysis, separated into his component parts, measured and named, replicated as a character and repositioned within a series of relational systems. Carraway's rage for order, and for knowledge, creates a chaotic monster: "Gatsby" animates an endlessly replicable and reducible object, one that forms in response and relation to variant concepts and then instantly reveals a disruptive capacity for misstatement and incongruity.

However, the Gatsby system, the Long Island hyperworld, does constitute an integrated and coherent entity. Gatsby, Carraway, the Buchanans, the guests—these are all component positions within an operating information system, one which states itself in its continual reconfiguration of intercomponent relations and contrives a cultural message about order and information in the process. The Gatsby system is finally about analysis and construction rather than Gatsby himself, and Carraway's inability completely to reintegrate his subject keeps the lines of communication open, powering the system through self-statement functions and enabling it successfully to absorb even the chaos of critical debate.

The Great Gatsby thus maintains an interactive relationship with the cultural hypersystem that contains it, participating in the construction of literary discourse and offering itself as a perturberant element in discourses about knowledge and information. Within those discourses, it insists upon the necessity of analytical explanation as it simultaneously proclaims the inadequacy of all explanatory projects. Further, it suggests that temporary collections and systematizations of information are ultimately our only connection with each other and our sole defense against chaos. It derides and feeds our desire for order.

Early in the novel, Carraway spies on Gatsby's silent communion with the night sky and the distant green light and then turns away. When he looks back toward Gatsby's position, he finds that Gatsby has vanished into the darkness (21–22). This seems to me to represent, elegantly and concisely, the analytic paradox: in this brief scene, the object of observation is fixed, evaluated, defined—and then escapes into chaos as soon as the gaze is lifted.

Gatsby's Party Revisited

*Modern thought is one that moves no
longer toward the never-completed
formation of Difference, but toward
the ever-to-be-accomplished unveiling
of the Same.*

—*Michel Foucault*
The Order of Things

None of the named party guests attends
Gatsby's funeral. Gatsby goes into the ground surrounded by
people whose names appear on no list: Carraway, Owl-eyes,
Mr. Gatz, a few servants, and the West Egg postman. And even
though the procession is delayed for half an hour, no one else
appears from East Egg, West Egg, or New York to swell the
pitiful number of Gatsby mourners.

The party guests overwhelm the funeral by virtue of their
absence; they crowd the cemetery with conspicuous neglect.
In a manifestation of severed social relations, they refuse
Gatsby's last act of hospitality and thereby transform their
categorical position from one of presence to absence.
The party guest list now registers absent mourners—containing identical names in a symmetrical structure that encodes a
violently reversed significance.The cohesion of the list tight-
ens under this alteration: the guests enact a unanimous similarity

here, and not one of them abandons the confines of the category. Even Klipspringer the boarder declines to attend—in spite of Carraway's concerted efforts to convince him.

Indeed, a disturbing and comprehensive sense of vacancy pervades the occasion: the mourners who do attend the funeral also suggest untenanted positions. Mr. Gatz appears on Long Island bearing tokens of Gatsby's long absence from name and home, young Jimmy's self-improvement schedule and a photograph of the mansion. Though supported "generously" by his son over the past years, he has nevertheless missed the party and has had no real contact with the replicant being buried under the name of Gatsby. Gatz and Gatsby are systemically noncongruent: each suggests an empty node occupied only by an imaginary other.

The second mourner, the man who once admired Gatsby's library, carries a similar suggestion of vacancy. Although Owl-eyes has a legitimate claim to inclusion in the party guest list, Carraway as narrator refuses acknowledgment of his status. Even his appearance at the funeral does not gain the owl-eyed man a name. Thus he is twice excluded from the record—and his position, though physically tenanted, has no denomination. Since his presence cannot therefore be fully expressed, he must eventually slip away into the abyss of the anonymous.

Finally, Carraway absents himself from the funeral by inhabiting multiscalar nodes. Since he occupies an external component as observer/narrator and an internal one as participant in the funeral, he is simultaneously present and absent from the graveside. The resultant turbulence destabilizes both positions—narrator and mourner—and calls into question the entire system of relations, hinting that relations with Gatsby are necessarily those of vacancy with void.

In the end, the problematics of the funeral foreground an essential emptiness, an absence initially defined by the transformed guest list and extended toward inscriptions of name and narrative function. This absence perhaps suggests a fundamental similarity which informs the entire system, a likeness of node to node in which subject and object positions are finally vacated.

It is a problematics of chaos, and one which deconstructs the system which encounters it: as everyone becomes relationally invisible, it becomes clear that no one was ever at the party at all.

Notes

chapter 1

Gatsby's Party

1. Indeed, the physical universe "as a total system can be interpreted as a continuum of sets of (spatio-temporal) relations between mass-energy events, [which are] the basis of all form and form characteristics" (Young 1987, 51).

chapter 2

Toxic Textual Events

1. According to Peter L. Cooper, a "scientist probing the micro world of isolated subatomic events sees not order and stability but rather displacement and discontinuity. . . . Yet a scientist viewing the macro world of fields and systems sees interrelation and reciprocity, integration and uniformity, order and continuity" (1983, 124–25).

2. Jeremy Campbell, in *Grammatical Man,* points out that closed systems eventually reach a point of equilibrium in which no further informational activity can take place. Open systems, on the other hand, reach a point of equifinality. This is a highly complex state the structures of which favor improbability; an equifinal system thus fluctuates from order to disorder, creating new rules and structures in the process (1982, 101–2).

3. Anything which interferes with the exchange of energy in a system is entropic. In a thermodynamic system, entropy is a loss of heat or of the distinction between hot and cold; in an infodynamic system, entropy is noise: nonsense, garbling of the message, uncommunicative language acts.

4. Fredric Jameson notes that contemporary pragmatists base their analyses of communication on evaluations of "language situations and games," which may (as in systems theory) promote transmission of messages or (as in game theory) subordinate message transference to the adversarial relationship between conversational "tricksters" (1984, xi).

5. Jean Baudrillard locates the beginnings of "simulation" in the "implosion" of meaning suggested by this very DNA model: here, he says, the gap between cause and effect, between subject and object, vanishes completely as the DNA nucleus *abolishes* relation by its "fantastic telescoping" of the roles of sender and receiver; this makes binarism, opposition, and differentiation impossible—so that meaning comes to reside in accurate replication rather than representation (1983, 57).

6. Norbert Wiener suggests that overload may lead to insanity. He notes that overload may be triggered "either by an excess in the amount of traffic to be carried, by a physical removal of channels for the carrying of traffic, or by the excessive occupation of such channels by undesirable systems of traffic" (1968, 151).

7. In his comprehensive study of DeLillo's novels, *In the Loop: Don DeLillo and the Systems Novel,* Tom LeClair points out that in "general scientific usage, 'white noise' is aperiodic sound with frequencies of random amplitude and random interval," while in music, the term refers to "the sound produced by all audible sound-wave frequencies sounding together . . ." (1987, 230). To LeClair, the first usage implies an acknowledgment of chaos; the second, a somewhat ironic and systematic ordering.

8. One naturally turns to Herman Melville for elucidation of the terrible nature of whiteness. In *Moby-Dick,* meditating upon the "whiteness of the whale," Ishmael notes that "by [white's] indefiniteness it shadows forth the heartless voids and immensities of the universe, and thus stabs us from behind with the thought of annihilation . . ." (1972, 295). It is precisely this void that DeLillo's title implies. Further, the title plays with the notion of sameness beneath difference, just as Ishmael does when he complains that it is only the action of light, itself colorless, that permits a perception of what we imagine is color (1972, 296).

9. Indeed, since the novel is contained in a visual medium available in bookstores if not the supermarket, one could very well consider Jack Gladney's narrative voice as the voice of the dead; one might think here of Kurt Vonnegut's *Galapagos* (1984), which is overtly narrated by a ghost.

10. Aside from their functional significance, these lists are meaningful because of their very improbability. Since language acts are controlled by rules and conventions (which help regulate the unpredictability of the system), anything which appears as a novelty within that context has informative value. Campbell notes that the familiarity of a context acts as a redundancy rule: it helps to reduce noise and ensure that the message gets through. However, something new in the context of what we know as "narrative" generates surprise, and to Campbell "[surprise] is virtually equivalent to information" (1982, 248).

11. The automobile, a ubiquitous presence in American life, is equally present in this novel, serving as dining room, place of meditation, and means of escape. In fact, it appears in a second list ("Toyota Corolla, Toyota Celica, Toyota Cressida") which Jack constructs after hearing daughter Steffie murmuring "Toyota Celica" in her sleep. He sees Steffie's utterance as evidence of the "Supranational names, computer-generated, more or less universally pronounceable" that are part of "every child's brain noise" (155).

12. Her courses, "Eating and Drinking: Basic Parameters" and "Posture," are designed to help ordinary citizens function in a world they can no longer understand; she separates and classifies essential activities and then teaches them to her students.

13. A useful concept here might be that of "cascades" of information. Douglas Hofstadter, in a discussion of the ways in which the brain stores information, notes that one bit of information may be used to "trigger" the release of other bits; in other words, a trigger word may permit other words or images to cascade down from an inaccessible location into accessible memory (1979, 664). What Babette performs here has a similar function; she has chunks of information stored together, so that they are mutually accessible via a traditional question trigger.

14. In DeLillo's 1976 novel *Ratner's Star,* scientist Lester Bolin turns to list making as a way of coping with his foreknowledge of imminent global catastrophe; one of those organizers who plans and directs his own activities by means of lists, Bolin now finds satisfaction in creating lists that have no task orientation and immediately *crossing out* items on the list (421). While this activity mimics the catastrophe that lies just ahead (the crossing out of human civilization), it also comments upon the pleasure to be derived from ordering: for Bolin, pleasure lies both in creation and destruction, in the attenuative process of listing, and in the immediacy of his response to his own lists.

15. A recent best seller, Richard Saul Wurman's *Information Anxiety* (1988), purports to advise Americans on ways to cope with the rapid increase in available knowledge and with technological changes that make "information" at once more accessible and more intimidating. Ted Mooney's 1981 novel, *Easy Travel to Other Planets,* describes an attack of "information sickness," the symptoms of which include "bleeding from the nose and ears, vomiting, deliriously disconnected speech, apparent disorientation, and the desire to touch everything" (34). Both of these books, one offering management strategies and one detailing physical breakdown, express contemporary concerns about the stress that accompanies an increase of information in the environment.

16. Kenneth Frampton, in an essay arguing against "universalized" urban architecture, uses as his epigraph a passage from Paul Ricoeur's *History and Truth* (1965); in this passage, Ricoeur, contemplating the paradoxical lowering of cultural diversity that accompanies the intermingling of cultures, says that worldwide "one finds the same bad movie, the same slot machines, the same plastic or aluminum atrocities" (16). This flattening of culture seems to be working on two levels: across cultures, we find the intrusion of mediocre categories of cultural artifacts; within cultures, we find a depressing sameness of items *within* categories.

17. Baudrillard would disagree; for him the truly American location is Disneyland, where infantilized thematic spaces conceal, by their overt claim to irreality, the fact that America itself is "no longer real, but of the order of the hyperreal and of simulation" (1983, 25).

18. When Murray tells Jack that "repression, compromise and disguise" are survival mechanisms, Jack says he takes care of himself by exercising, and an anonymous source comments "Tegrin, Denorex, Selsun Blue" (289). When Winnie Richards tells Jack that fear is both a survival mechanism and a border that *defines* life, Jack thinks "Clorets, Velamints, Freedent" (229). Clearly, the emotional awareness Murray and Winnie encourage in Jack triggers in him a sort of supermarket-shelf response, an automatic tendency to link emotional and spiritual concerns with the type of bodily awareness recommended in television commercials.

19. And, of course, the mall. It seems completely and wonderfully appropriate that developers saw fit to name a shopping center in Huntington, New York, the "Walt Whitman Mall."

20. Allen Ginsberg aptly links Whitman to the supermarket in his poem "A Supermarket in California." "In my hungry fatigue, and shopping for images," he writes, "I went into the neon fruit supermarket, dreaming of [Whitman's] enumerations" (1984, 136). It is not only images that Ginsberg can shop for in Whitman's enumerations but also versions of American reality. Whitman sees America as a cornucopia of realities, a wealth of opportunities taken or passed by; Ginsberg, in turn, sees Whitman as a supermarket of images, Whitman's poetry as a place to shop for ways to speak of America.

21. This sort of inattentiveness seems to be suggested in the list "Krylon, Rust-Oleum, Red Devil" (159), which appears in Jack's account of his family's escape from an "airborne toxic event," the cloud of Nyodene Derivative. Knowing the *names* of paints in this context seems much less important than knowing that paints are *toxic*. Further, this list of homely toxins (available in the local supermarket or hardware store) points out that there is simply nowhere to hide: no refugee center is truly safe from the toxic effects of American life.

22. This may represent the ultimate end of an open system: a homeostasis in which all energy is regulated, all information is processed, and there is no longer any movement toward greater complexity but only reproductions of the system or an increase in extent (Wilden 1980, 139).

23. In a universe where language is not systematic but ludic, Jack could change the rules, making noise a token of power or object of desire rather than a sign of systemic breakdown. DeLillo operates on the metasystemic level, and his reconstruction of chaos is perhaps similar to the language game Jean-François Lyotard has in mind when he says, "a move can be made for the sheer pleasure of its invention: what else is involved in that labor of language harassment undertaken by popular speech and by literature" (1984, 10).

24. Cooper suggests that in Pynchon's *Gravity's Rainbow* the gravity of the narrative "recycles the fragments, detritus, and exhausted materials of our culture" into "new combinations and associations" (1983, 214).

chapter 3

The Narrative Supersystem

1. Consider the supermarket system in *White Noise;* the rearrangement of items on the shelves is chaotic because it alters the relation between one component (products) and another (shoppers); this must be quickly countered or the system will collapse. Two options are open: (1) reestablish the relation by either returning to the old shelf order or retraining the shoppers, or (2) reconfigure the relationship by declaring "shopper confusion" legitimate. If no action is taken, the supermarket ceases to function as (to be) a supermarket.

2. An attractor is the force that moves a system in a particular direction; for closed systems conforming to traditional thermodynamic theory, that attractor is entropy. Any system has a preferred state from which it will not move without outside impulsion; a system will naturally move from an initial state to this preferred final state (Prigogine and Stengers 1984, 121–22).

3. Since the entropic trend of a closed system cannot be reversed, the direction of time within that system is fixed toward a future of maximum entropy (Prigogine and Stengers 1984, 119). In an open system, however, entropy flows in both directions, which suggests a suspension of time within the open system and perhaps even a reversal of time's arrow.

4. Systems theorists Francisco Varela and Humberto Maturana describe a hierarchy of open systems. An allonomous system, at the lowest level, is defined by its relationship with, interaction with, or use by another larger system. An autonomous system is self-defining and does not depend upon a subsidiary relationship to another system for its identity. And an auto-poietic system, at the highest level of the hierarchy, is not only self-defining but self-producing as well (Paulson 1988, 126–67).

5. A narrative system is also thermodynamically open; it accepts and uses both light energy and the reader's psycho-physical energy to perform its structural processes.

6. David Porush, in *The Soft Machine* (1985), says if "we think of the literary text as a device intended to represent 'some internal state' of the author or to produce certain desired states in the reader, we bring fiction into cybernetic territory" (21).

7. William R. Paulson agrees that a literary text is an "artificially autonomous object," one that is granted its autonomy by convention (1988, 135). And he would contend that because this is so, the systemic coherence of its internal structure must ultimately deconstruct or exhibit the intervention of its creator (1988, 142). However, on a metaphorical level, where critical discourse takes place, the text's coherence never quite collapses because it can recuperate itself as a reconstructed system which includes the aporiatic gap or the creative hand as a *component* of the system.

8. Ludwig von Bertalanffy, in *General System Theory* (1968), defines structure as the "order of parts" and function as the "order of processes" (27).

9. Ervin Laszlo notes that systems have a natural tendency to merge with other systems to form supersystems that are extremely complex in form and function; a system is therefore a "coordinating interface" in a hierarchy (1972, 67). Hierarchically arranged systems maintain coherence (on the subsystemic level) even when the supersystem is reduced to its parts; this has an obvious survival value not possessed by nonhierarchic aggregations, which break apart and scatter when reduced (1972, 68).

10. Varela and Maturana term this configuration "structural coupling"; here, two autonomous systems interact by virtue of being environmental factors (perturbations) for each other, "in a manner that establishes an interlocked, mutually structuring, mutually triggering domain" of components and processes (quoted in Paulson 1988, 129).

11. Von Bertalanffy points out that any "system as an entity which can be investigated in its own right must have boundaries, either spatial or dynamic. Strictly speaking, spatial boundaries exist only in naive observation, and all boundaries are ultimately dynamic" (1968, 215).

12. *Internal* plasticity permits some flexibility in the configuration of relationships between the parts of the system and in the inhabitation of structural nodes. The location of nodes and the timely fulfillment of functions may be specified, but only in generic terms: specific tenants and methods then establish a structural personality, which may or may not have consequences for the overall configuration of the system (Laszlo 1972, 113–14). New relationships may eventually form in response to the idiosyncracies of tenants; new functions may be needed in response to alterations in method.

13. See his extended discussion of systems at the subatomic, chemical, biological, and social levels in *The Systems View of the World* (1972). He contends that natural systems at all these levels exhibit autonomous functions as invariants: *gestalt* structuration, self-definition and restructuration, and hierarchic interfacing.

14. Porush describes the text as "a model, something constructed with the materials of a systematic code . . . and with a systematic relationship among its various parts, all designed to represent the functioning of an intelligence or world view. . . . [If] the text is viewed *as a model of the techniques or methods that created it,* which in turn implies a measure of self-awareness or self-reflexiveness in the text, then we can almost speak of the text as an artificial intelligence device" (1985, 21).

15. See Varela's *Principles of Biological Autonomy* (1979).

16. Paulson makes extensive use of this Varela term, which refers to a system that is "both autonomous and continuously self-producing or self-creating"; a recursive relation exists between the processes and components of such a system: the processes depend upon and create the system's components, and the components depend upon and realize the processes (1988, 125).

17. Of course, since some nodes in a narrative supersystem may be filled by humans, attempts at such representation are paradoxically possible. However, any human must, at the moment of representation, stand *outside* its position in the narrative supersystem in order to gain a metasystemic viewpoint. No subsystem in a supersystem is sufficient for representation of the total system, just as no single organ contains sufficient information to create a representation of its human host.

18. Once a system reaches an equilibrium state, only small brief movements away from that state will be made; the system will fluctuate around that equilibrium state, with compensation for this variation coming from the great number of simultaneous events (which tend to remove the variation statistically) (Prigogine and Stengers 1984, 124).

19. Paulson begins his work on noise with the assumption that (1) "literature is a noisy transmission channel that assumes its noise so as to become something other than a transmission channel [i.e., an autonomous system]"; and (2) "literature, so constituted, functions as the noise of culture, as a perturbation or source of variety in the circulation and production of discourse and ideas" (1988, ix). In other words, literary noise, by its presence as a disruptive factor in the cultural system, forces the reconfiguration of cultural discourse structures and the redefinition of literary noise as cultural information.

20. Hierarchical positioning does not indicate relative importance, merely a change in scale.

21. Mapping involves the creation of a conceptual model in which the steps of a process under explanation are exactly reproduced as transforms of input; relations must remain constant throughout (Bateson 1972, 407).

chapter 4

Surprise Roast

1. Wiener notes that the status of mechanism is not limited to inanimate cogs and wheels; he says that whatever *"is used as an element in the machine, is in fact an element in the machine"* (1967, 254, italics in original). Thus, a person used as an element in an information or communication mechanism is as much a part of the system as any fiber-optic cable or satellite dish.

2. Porush describes paranoia as "a sort of *epistemology gone wild . . .*" (1985, 107).

3. Like Pynchon himself, whose reclusive nature is, according to Edward Mendelson, "alien" to modern literary culture (and thus presumably outside the law) (1986, 38).

4. Mikhail Bakhtin links seriousness to official structure, noting that it is "infused with elements of fear, weakness, humility, submission, falsehood, hypocrisy . . . violence, intimidation, threats, [and] prohibitions" (1984, 94).

5. Wiener notes that an increased cybernetic technology implies a more sophisticated State mechanism for governance, one which assures the success of the State in any human gaming situation; this forces a player other than the State (or here, System) to choose between two options, either "immediate ruin, or planned co-operation" (1967, 245).

6. Bakhtin notes that a feast has an essentially temporal quality, that it calls attention either to the cosmic cycle or to "biological or historical timeliness" (1984, 9). A feast, existing outside mundane time, serves to emphasize the relationship of participants to the cyclical or linear time frame from which the feast has temporarily escaped. Similarly, Pynchon's Zone exists in a period of non-time that represents an extended and highly potential present from which a new history, a new order, must eventually emerge.

7. An alternative use of the preexisting system would be for a character to ride the "network of all plots" to freedom, using the plot structure created in the Zone as a "transit system" (603) as Slothrop hopes to do; unfortunately, such an escape requires the maintenance of a "minimum state of grace," which seems unattainable for Slothrop and his cohorts.

8. Alliteration forces a link between two words, here working against a cultural proscription that insists on the separation of food and the body. Further, I would suggest that the alliteration itself works to make these dishes particularly disgusting, allowing the *sound* of the name to linger just a bit too long on the tongue, permitting the speaker/reader to savor the name of the dish in a way that a nonalliterative menu would not.

9. Bertrand Russell's theory of logical types "asserts that no class can, in formal logical or mathematical discourse, be a member of itself; that a class of classes cannot be one of the classes which are its members . . ." (Bateson 1972, 280).

10. See Pig Bodine's explanation of the expression "Shit from Shinola" (687–88), which centers on the importance of categoric distinctions; he speculates that the expression *implies* "wildly different categories" which simply cannot coexist, but that in fact the two not only share the same consistency and color but also coexist in the men's toilet at Roseland. He suggests that the white men whose shoes are shined with Shinola fear shit because it marks the presence of death, the "stiff and rotting corpse itself inside the white man's warm and private own *asshole* . . ." (688), a fear exacerbated by the coexistence of two mutually exclusive things, life and death.

11. In similar fashion, cafeteria rituals from my own childhood involved groups of initiates who were able to recite (and withstand the imagery of) such rhymes as:

> Great big gobs of greasy grimy gopher guts,
> Mutilated monkey meat,
> Little baby birdies' beaks.
> Great big gobs of greasy grimy gopher guts,
> And me without a spoon.

Those who flinched were effectually expelled from the group; those who could create new rhymes rose to eminence.

12. Mendelson says that like its predecessors, *The Divine Comedy, Gargantua and Pantagruel, Don Quixote, Faust, Moby-Dick,* and *Ulysses, Gravity's Rainbow* is an encyclopedic narrative located in a position of illegality, in this case through violations of literary decorum rather than through clerical or other social interdiction. He notes that Seaman Bodine and Roger Mexico's "verbal disruption of officialdom at the dinner table" is only one of many "stomach-turning pages" in the book, and he remarks that critics' failure to recognize and discuss such scenes disregards the "unmistakable power" of Pynchon's language to "shock and disgust, without ever allowing itself to be dismissed as infantilism or mere noise" (1986, 38).

13. Cooper calls the efforts of the Counterforce "juvenile and finally ineffectual pranks" (1983, 109) and suggests that such actions cannot prevent the eventual co-optation of the Counterforce into the Firm (just as the subversive intent of the American Counterculture movement in the late sixties did not keep it from being absorbed into the mainstream). However, the escape of Roger Mexico and Seaman Bodine leaves them free to continue their efforts against the System. One might think of Panurge's escape from the Turks' roasting spit in François Rabelais' *Gargantua and Pantagruel* (see book 2, chapter 14); he escapes only to find himself beset by a pack of hungry dogs, a situation which requires yet another escape to ensure Panurge's continuance as a counterforce against sobriety. Just so does each effort against the System have only local and temporary effect, yet that is perhaps all one would wish to have, lest one become tempted to try global solutions.

14. This recurrence of the banana figure has been interpreted as part of a narrative strategy of paranoia. Richard Poirer notes that the "persistent paranoia of all the important characters [in the novel] invests any chance detail with the power of an omen" (quoted in Stark 1980, 32); John Stark believes that the bananas gain a heightened significance from their recurrence, increasing the reader's own paranoia and causing her to fear that the bananas have a deeper metaphorical import that she has failed to recognize.

15. Roger Henkle calls the banana a "classic phallic symbol" which (unlike the rocket) is "a rich and natural thing . . .; nutritious, fragrant, contributing to man's health and not his destruction" (1983, 273).

16. Indeed, one might say that the war is critiqued as well as consumed in the shapes appearing at breakfast: the molded bananas contrast a rampant British lion against an egg-battered French toast, the blancmange suggests a substandard war effort by quoting from Clausewitz, and the bananas flambé remind us that covert operations lie beneath the overt conduct of hostilities.

17. The image of the banana is powerful partly because it is so unexpected; Elaine Safer rightly considers the Banana Breakfasts to be "incongruous with a war situation" (1988, 96). They are anomalous (and therefore highly informative about their context) in an economy of scarcity.

18. Stark speculates that the early morning scene at Pirate Prentice's apartment is influenced by "[Wolfgang] Kohler's experiments with apes (*The Mentality of Apes*) and . . . Robert Yerkes's experiments with chimpanzees (*Chimpanzees: A Laboratory Colony*)" because of the "omnipresent bananas and the characters' subhuman actions" (1980, 94). This would certainly conform to the novel's concern with human experimentation and behavior modification and would link the chimpanzees' escape from Frau Gnahb's boat to various other escapes and acts of resistance to outside control that begin to occur late in the novel.

19. Henkle notes that the Candy Drill parodies the "notoriously eccentric English sweet tooth" as it unites the important themes of sex and war in such delicacies as the gelatin earthquake bomb and the licorice bazooka (1983, 274).

20. Italo Calvino, writing about the use of myth in narrative, says that the "primitive tribe's first story-teller" created his tale not in order to convey a story but as an exercise in combination and permutation, an exercise designed to test the limits of language (1981, 75).

chapter 5

Patterns within Patterns

1. Indeed, as Paul Young points out, the "word information derives from the Latin *informare* . . . meaning to give form, shape, or character to . . ." (1987, 6). This etymological link serves him well in his argument that the nature of information is essentially formal, i.e., that it involves the formal coding of and transmission of complementary and significant forms.

2. *Equivocation* is information generated at the source but not transmitted to the receiver; it is part of the total information pool at the source and is simply held in potential unless it enters the system as noise (Dretske 1981, 19). The data which are Gatsby related but not selected for transmission are equivocal.

3. A system faced with an increase in information input must either (1) increase channel capacity or (2) organize the information to permit parallel processing (Resnikoff 1989, 94). Parallel processing involves the "subdivison of a problem into smaller constituents which can be solved independently and simultaneously"; the recombination of the (solved) constituent problems results in the solution of the original problem (Resnikoff 1989, 111). One might think of narrative strategy as an exercise in parallel processing.

4. Young points out that *structure, configuration, conformation,* and *shape* all refer to external spatial characteristics, while *pattern* refers to temporal repetitions of structure or behavior; however, these definitions are united by an underlying concept of relation, which is what finally determines both form and information (1987, 48).

5. This process, in physicomathematical terms, applies to "systems whose behavior is determined by general laws that are instantiated by the prescription of specified constraints on particular parts of the system" (Resnikoff 1989, 165).

6. A representational structure acquires its meaning from the information that led to its development; thereafter, it confers on later uses of the structure its own semantic content even when these later uses (or tokens) *do not* have the same informational content (Dretske 1981, 193). This concept formation principle simply means that the learning situation, or the interpretive situation, affects subsequent encounters with the information structure even when it appears with completely novel content.

7. Even if a pattern is unfamiliar, its conformation to a recognizable set of relations (and its difference from non-relational data) at least alerts us to some formal or structural coherence, and therefore to the presence of information.

8. That some of these patterns imply list structures as containers ironically reflects Gatsby's own attempts to structure his behavior by means of lists.

9. Self-similarity (or recurrent patterns observable at variant scales of measurement) is common in complex systems (see Mandelbrot 1983 and Barnsley and Demko 1986).

10. Similarly, Young points out that "information" refers to (1) the probability distribution of a range of messages which are (2) "unambiguously understood" by the sender and receiver, out of which the reception of any one message (3) reduces the level of uncertainty in the receiver in an amount correlated with the probability of having received that particular message; in other words, in communication theory, information does not equal meaning, it equals a reduction in the uncertainty of the universe (1987, 7).

11. Here, Atlan speaks of noise that enters an intended or "sent" message in either the encoding process or the transmission process (see Atlan 1979).

12. Bateson notes that patterns imply complementary patterns of interpretive skills; the meaning of a pattern is lost to the world if the ability to decode the pattern has died out (1979, 46). In Walter M. Miller, Jr.'s *A Canticle for Leibowitz* (1976), for instance, the grocery list preserved by the monks who survive the nuclear holocaust simply cannot be interpreted correctly; although it is clear to the monks that the list is a pattern encoding meaning, that meaning is lost to them because the structure "shopping list" is as unrecognizable as the concepts of pastrami, canned kraut, and bagels. As an undecipherable relic, the list is finally accorded religious significance and preserved through the centuries. This suggests that information cannot really be stored.

13. Information may be transferred via *complementary* forms (equivalent sets of relations) rather than by the copying of form (Young 1987, 71); for example, a telephone conversation takes place because the wires carry coded complementary forms (which are subsequently decoded, producing a facsimile of the original input), not because they actually carry voices.

14. For Fred Dretske, information is *not equal to* meaning; he notes that a message can "mean" something without carrying information. To qualify as "information" a message must have truth value; it must contain something a properly equipped receiver can assimilate as knowledge (1981, 44–47). Consequently, a lie (or a believed but inaccurate statement) does not qualify as information under Dretske's definition.

15. A system's awareness of or perception of this difference is subject to the threshold of the information-gathering mechanism involved; the actual difference may lie outside or beneath the range of the system's observation (Bateson 1979, 29).

16. In the analysis of difference, one must look at the "dichotomy between pattern and quantity" as well as the "dichotomy between continuity and discontinuity" (Bateson 1979, 169). The data must be interrogated to see whether a new category is established by a difference in size or by a difference in pattern, by a move to a new and discrete level or at some point on a gradual scale.

17. The semantic content of any statement can be identified with its "outermost information shell" or with that bit of information converted into its most completely digitalized form; other digital and analog representations of the information may be nested inside this shell: for instance, "x is a cat" also contains the information that "x is a mammal," "x is a four-legged animal," "x has a tail," etc. (Dretske 1981, 178, 184).

18. A structure identifying x as a cat can be developed *without* the accompanying information that "x has a tail" if the learning (or construction) situation is properly controlled (Dretske 1981, 221).

19. Significantly, the list is itself inscribed upon the blank portions of an old timetable.

Two Hundred Whores

1. "A fatal fool. A high-toned fool. A natural fool." See *Gargantua and Pantagruel,* book 3, chapter 38.

2. By the time this list appears, protagonist Ebenezer Cooke has placed himself precisely within the Rabelaisian tradition by contemplating the advantages and disadvantages of various sorts of bum-wipes after the manner of Gargantua in his youth (see book 1, chapter 13). The list of epithets is also Rabelaisian; Bakhtin notes, in *Rabelais and His World,* that "lengthy strings of names and military terms and the accumulation of epithets . . . were common in the fifteenth and sixteenth centuries" (1984, 177). The appearance of such lists in *Gargantua and Pantagruel* clearly responds to this practice; at the same time it establishes for later writers a literary convention of excess. Barth's lengthy string of names follows the antiphonal pattern of Pantagruel's and Panurge's discussion of the virtues of the fool Triboulet (book 3, chapter 38) and actually contains 228 synonyms for "whore."

3. *The Sot-Weed Factor,* ever a site of contradiction, forces me to refute myself: there are, in fact, 1600 virgins in the novel. A pirate reports that these virgins (Moors bound for Mecca) were overtaken by pirates and lost their maidenheads in a massive rape taking place over a "day and a night" (253); the tale is told during the rape of the whore ship *Cyprian,* during which Ebenezer himself nearly loses his virginity. Still, these unfortunate Moors have only one name, "virgin," and thus cannot compete in any sort of nominative enumeration with the "whores."

4. The delight turns to dismay when Burlingame surpasses his instructor by finding twenty-one Hudribrastic rhymes for "Colonelling" (382). Ebenezer then proposes a contest of "perfect" matches for words, which he appears to win with the unrhymable "month"; however, Ebenezer is only allowed a short time to gloat because Burlingame reverses this loss by using the rules of grammar to prove that "onth" is a word and hence a perfect match for "month" (386).

5. Ebenezer himself has borne several names during the course of the novel, including Henry Cook, Bertrand Burton, and Edward Cooke—and Henry Burlingame, Bertand Burton, and John McEvoy have all borne *his* name. Gerhard Joseph points out that Ebenezer is an imitation of an imitation of an archetype (Ebenezer Cooke of Joseph Andrews of Pamela) (1970, 30). These seem to me to be two versions of the character *as* list.

6. The joy with which the whores enter into this naming game seems to support Bakhtin's notion of the inherent duality of marketplace language. He argues that this language "abuses while praising and praises while abusing" (1984, 415) and suggests that this duality stems from a recognition of a generative cycle: the impulse toward rebirth implied in every form of death and the potential for, indeed *inevitability* of, transformation. In Bakhtin's view, then, every word of abuse is poised on the brink of praise, and an excess of either calls attention to the opposition contained within each.

7. In the universe of this list system, Ebenezer's first comment is not turbulent; it is outside the observation scale of systemic functioning. His second comment, lexically equal to the information comprising the whores' list, *is* an environmental challenge; it is absorbed into the lexicon and thus gains peripheral association with the list (at least in its role as narratological unit).

8. If such a long thin list suggests that it is gender marked as male, then the paragraph list, which encloses, enfolds, and perhaps conceals its members might be the female of the list species.

9. Heide Ziegler, in *John Barth,* argues that Barth's "list of dirty names" draws the reader's attention toward language and away from the "real thing," the nature of eros (1987, 32). I would say that the list precisely does not obscure the reality of eros but rather reveals it as inherently *constructed* by language.

10. Bakhtin points out that translators of *Gargantua* frequently added the names of local games to the enumeration of games played by Gargantua after dinner (book 1, chapter 22). The most impressive contribution was by the German translator Johann Fischart who added 372 games and dance tunes to his 1575 edition (1984, 231).

11. And here Barth provides Ebenezer with an extranarrative opportunity to achieve at least one goal: the interruption of the whore's dialogue. For although the whores do ignore Ebenezer's attempts at interruption *within* the narrative, the list itself is quite effectively interrupted by the long lines that contain the narration of Ebenezer's attempts.

12. Walkiewicz notes that Hugh Kenner (1962) talks of exhaustion as a "comedy of the Inventory" which is "created when a finite set is circumscribed and all of its members enumerated. This strategy . . . has the advantage of making exhaustiveness a virtue, for it generates joy by satisfying the reader's desire for completeness" (1986, 48). In this scene the reader's satisfaction is clearly opposed to Ebenezer's discomfort in the face of completeness, and the tension between the two opposing desires surely increases the reader's joy.

13. Smith's journal makes frequent note of Burlingame's corpulence and excessive appetite; however, *The Privie Journall of Sir Henry Burlingame* (encountered early in the novel) recounts a "Gargantuan" feast served up by Chief Powhatan, at which Smith gorges himself and Lord Burlingame is "unable to keep a morsel on his stomach" (151).

14. The Burlingame men seem fated to serve always as proxies: Henry Burlingame III claims that his sexual relations with Ebenezer's twin, Anna, were conducted only as proxy for Ebenezer himself (490), and Henry's brother Billy Rumbly discovers he has served Anna as proxy for Henry (663).

15. There are at least 48 different items served, including the vegetables and berries served during the meat course.

16. The variety of means for killing and preparing foods implies a rich and active culture; the intensity and productivity of native life is here contrasted with the Smith company's rather tenuous relationship with the Maryland wilderness.

17. Here we find further mirroring of Smith and Burlingame. Burlingame's *Privie Journall* reveals that he learned the secret of the eggplant from Smith, who used its power to penetrate the "stout" hymen of Pocahontas.

18. Barth, in *The End of the Road* (1988), quotes the first proposition of Wittgenstein's *Tractatus:* "The world is everything that is the case" (76).

19. Barth does, in fact, go on to exhaust the problem of balance in *Giles Goat-Boy* (1987).

c h a p t e r **7**

Inside the List

1. Cooper believes Pynchon provides examples of lists that have no assumption of coherence; he says that a Pynchon narrator will often "begin listing things so as to reveal an attitude toward them but not a conceptual framework that can order them into any kind of logical or meaningful progression" (1983, 217). I would argue that the attitude *is* the relational substructure that forces coherence upon the list.

2. See Jorge Luis Borges (1974).

3. Michel Foucault points out that the forcing of the fabulous Chinese animals into categories "localizes their powers of contagion" (1973, xv). Contained within this conceptual framework, the fabulous animals are prevented from association with the real, a rhetorical move that protects the integrity of episte-mological boundaries.

4. William Gass feels that Foucault misses the point of Borges's list, that the proper *site* of the list is one of logical error: the invocation of nonexclusive categories, the excesses of reduction and failure to generalize, and the suppression of actual distinction construct a list that *seems* to be about animals but is really about logic (1985, 123).

5. If we consider Gatsby a guest at his own parties, we might use him as an example of a categorical *generator,* a cen-tral member which, by means of relational rules, provides motivation for other members to enter the category (Lakoff 1987, 24). The formation that results from the activity of a generator is a radial category; like some kinship groups, the members are conventionally linked and motivated by principles of extension validated by social conceptions of the central member (Lakoff 1987, 91).

6. A "'property' is not something objectively in the world independent of any being; it is rather . . . an *interactional prop-erty*—the result of our interactions as part of our physical and cultural environments given our bodies and our cognitive apparatus" (Lakoff 1987, 51). Here, place of origin has no significance independent of the list; being from West Egg is not a classificatory selector until the list frame is in place and internal clustering is in process.

7. Rosch identifies a "basic level" of categorization with-in any taxonomy which correlates with high-level performance and/or primary organic experience in similarity identification, image construction, application of motor function, speed of recognition, name acquisition in children, quantity of infor-mation, and the default position for neutral contextualization (Lakoff 1987, 46). In a taxonomy filled by vessel/glass/snifter, "glass" occupies the basic level as the member we routinely encounter, the one we recognize most easily, the one children learn first, and the one around which our general categorical information clusters. In Carraway's hierarchy, "party guest" occupies the basic level, and everything else is either superordinate or subordinate to that taxonomic position.

8. Carraway provides information about personal history in eleven cases and about party history (or party behavior) in ten.

9. In the process, Carraway's list takes on a new definition, moving away from categorical intention (naming the guests) toward a representation of particular cognitive experiences: Carraway's recollection processes and his representational strategies, both of which extend identification in directions other than naming.

10. Lévi-Strauss points out that "science as a whole is based on the distinction between the contingent and the necessary, this being also what distinguishes event and structure" (1966, 21).

11. Gertrude Stein, explaining her composition of *The Making of Americans,* notes that the essential similarity of the continuous present tends toward list construction:

> It was all so nearly alike it must be different
> and it is different, it is natural that if everything
> is used and there is a continuous present and a
> beginning again and again if it is all so alike it
> must be simply different and everything simply
> different was the natural way of creating it then.

> In this natural way of creating it then that it
> was simply different everything being alike it was
> simply different, this kept on leading one to lists.
> (1962, 519)

12. Further, since the included or positioned item gains authority (and categorical stability) from the list itself, the property enabling such a classification may be accorded unwarranted importance (Goody 1977, 105–6).

13. Systems theory "shows that digitalization is always necessary when communication crosses the boundary between different states or different systems—and that it creates the boundary by doing so" (Wilden 1980, 28).

14. A theory promoted in the eighteenth century by J. B. Robinet held that "everything that has form has a shell onto-genesis, and life's principal effort is to make shells" (Bachelard 1969, 112).

15. Stephen Barney notes that narratable order requires (1) aliorelativity (an arrangement of two or more items); (2) connexity (a common principle relating items); (3) asymmetry (a fixed nonreversible relation); and (4) transitivity (reliably asymmetrical relations across sequence). Lists, however, may be symmetrical and intransitive; items may be reversible and equivalent (1982, 192).

16. Written lists date back to the very beginning of writing, to about 3000 B.C.E. in Sumeria; early examples are clearly administrative, listing property and accounts (Goody 1977, 82).

17. In his essay "And," Gass provides a list of lists based on principles of command, desire, collection, chaos, and convenience. These lists, he says, are (1) encountered in fact and reproduced in writing; (2) aligned with an external concept; or (3) generated in response to a natural or preexisting order (1985, 117).

18. Elaine Scarry notes that the genealogical inventories in Genesis contain "a tone of triumph and self-assurance that is simply awesome [and that some] of the scale and magnitude of the initial creation itself is gradually implicated in the slow but increasingly inevitable transformation of two people into 'a people'" (1985, 185). Goody links both divine and secular genealogy to the administrative chronicle and the subsequent development of "history" (1977, 91).

19. Goody identifies three kinds of nominal lists: (1) the nominal roll (members who are entitled to be or should be present, (2) the selective list (members self-enrolled or otherwise chosen), and (3) the retrospective list (members actually present) (1977, 130).

20. The result is what Gaston Bachelard calls "intimate immensity," a perspective with a peculiar intensity (1969, 193).

21. In speaking of an apparent distinction between the totalizing impulse of analytical reason and fragmentalizing impulse of dialectical reason, Lévi-Strauss suggests that this opposition is only a temporary one, a gap immediately bridged by dialectical attempts at transcendence of analytical stasis (1966, 246).

22. Gabriele Schwab, although she would call the work one of ecology rather than encyclopedology, like Mendelson sees in texts such as *Gravity's Rainbow* an act of unification (1986, 99–100); for Schwab, however, the initiation of the narrative does not begin with anatomization of a culture but with "interrelation of commonly isolated areas of experience that convey the notion of history"—a process requiring, as Bateson would suggest, an acknowledgment that categories of order are conventional and convenient abstractions rather than actual subdivisions existing in nature.

| chapter **8**
Stuffed Parrots

1. This process tends to circulate culturally validated forms throughout the system, since the reception node, like the channel and the sender, is already informed by the same conceptual and epistemological constraints that define the data pool.

2. Shortly after Fitzgerald's death in 1940, Edmund Wilson collected Fitzgerald's notebooks, letters, and essays and published them as *The Crack-Up* (1945). The publisher's blurb on the book-jacket claims that this is "the nearest thing to an autobiography that Fitzgerald ever wrote." Wilson's own prefatory remarks suggest that he too considers that this collation of fragments forms a relatively coherent picture of Fitzgerald, that biography can somehow be captured if enough documentary items can be assembled in one place.

3. The location of Braithwaite's text is what Linda Hutcheon would call a heterocosm, a fictional world with its own rules (1980, 90). Braithwaite's museum contains within it sets of relations and construction principles borrowed from two systemically connected interior heterocosms, *Madame Bovary* and *Bouvard and Pécuchet.*

4. "What do we need to know?" he says. "Not everything. Everything confuses. Directness also confuses. The full-face portrait staring back at you hypnotises" (108).

5. Hutcheon points out that the structure and theme of *Madame Bovary* foreground the abyss standing between language and reality, forcing a relationship of reader to text rather than reader to world via text (1980, 150). Braithwaite's structure mirrors that gap although his desire is for a textual explanation of his own personal trauma.

6. Paul De Man feels that the "interest of autobiography . . . is not that it reveals reliable self-knowledge—it does not—but that it demonstrates in a striking way the impossibility of closure and of totalization (that is, the impossibility of coming into being) of all textual systems made up of tropological substitutions" (1984, 71).

7. Roland Barthes, in approving the essentially fragmentary method, notes that "with Flaubert, for this first time, discontinuity is no longer exceptional . . . [that Flaubert has] a way of cutting, of perforating discourse *without rendering it meaningless*" (1975, 8–9). However, inside their own text, Bouvard and Pécuchet do manage to render discourse meaningless by separating it from context; their experience is not one of *jouissance* but of a pointless trek through a textual wilderness.

8. See Baudrillard (1970).

9. Donato notes that "having begun with the dream and hope of a total, finite, rational domain of knowledge, [Bouvard and Pécuchet] come to realize that not only is knowledge as a given totality unavailable but that also any act of totalization is by definition incomplete, infinite, and everywhere marked by accident, chance, and randomness . . ." (1986, 207).

10. The objects in the museum are "twice removed" (spatially and temporally) from their significatory relationship with reality, and thus "signify only by arbitrary and derived associations" (Donato 1986, 211).

11. Donato points to a fundamental naiveté in the assumptions beneath museum collections; the "set of objects of the Museum displays," he says, is "sustained only by the fiction that they somehow constitute a coherent representational universe. The fiction is that a repeated metonymic displacement of fragment for totality, object to label, series of objects to series of labels, can still produce a representation which is somehow adequate to a nonlinguistic universe. Such a fiction is the result of an uncritical belief in the notion that ordering and classifying, [and] the spatial juxtaposition of fragments, can produce a representational understanding of the world" (1986, 211).

12. Georges Cuvier noted in *Recherches sur les ossements fossiles* (1834-36) that as an archeological antiquarian he "found it necessary to learn . . . to restore these monuments of past [geological] revolutions and to decode their sense; it was my task to collect and to put together in their original order the fragments which composed them, to reconstruct the antique creatures to which these fragments belonged; to reproduce them conserving their proportions and their characteristics . . ." (quoted in Donato 1986, 213).

13. Hassan points out that the "varieties of critical experience are endless . . . desiring, reading, acting (which here includes making) . . . are all fragments of an autobiography, itself but a sentient reed in the universe" (1987, 147). Braithwaite criticizes academics for their exploitation of their subjects and their archeologic approach; he misses the essentially autobiographic nature of all critical activity, something Hassan here recognizes and even valorizes.

14. As Pécuchet says, "everything decays, crumbles, changes form. Creation is put together in such an elusive and transitory fashion; we should do better to take up something else!" (Flaubert 1976, 99).

15. Bouvard and Pécuchet despair of accounting for all these subsystems; they cry out, "So many systems confuse you. Metaphysics is useless. One can live without it" (Flaubert 1976, 209).

chapter 9

The Cultural Hypersystem

1. Objects of discourse are determined by (1) an examination or mapping of the "surfaces of their emergence" (where differences are accorded status), (2) a description of "the authorities of delimitation" (who is allowed to determine difference), and (3) an analysis of the "grids of specification" (the systems of division and classification) (Foucault 1972, 41–42). Likewise, the identity of a hypersystem can be discovered through mapping, deciphering of codes that permit differentiation, and an analysis of component positions. These lead to a statement of relations, which is essentially the name of the system.

2. Bateson suggests that nature is also subject to connection by metapattern; patterns are repeated up through and across species, and these patterns are themselves linked by a greater pattern (1979, 11).

3. Foucault points out that the statement (like the name of the system) has a unique place that is not a position of usurpation, that is not occupied at the expense of other, suppressed statements. Rather, its place is dependent upon the network that creates its location; the statement's position is one of isolation in the midst of dispersion (1972, 119).

4. A discursive formation may be analyzed from four directions: "formation of objects, formation of the subjective positions, formation of concepts, formation of strategic choices" (Foucault 1972, 116).

5. This critical project begins such a hierarchization in its figuration of narrative functions and confirms it by creating a taxonomy that implies ascending structural levels in its application of labels such as hyposystem, subsystem, system, supersystem, and now hypersystem.

6. N. Katherine Hayles notes that Foucault's concept of the *episteme* implies that "different sites within a given cultural period are self-similar" (1990, 218). Consequently, local-to-global symmetry facilitates movement up and down the scale. Highly symmetrical structures are very fragile, however; their configuration facilitates and amplifies intrasystemic perturbation, rippling alterations throughout the cultural entity.

7. Hayles suggests that chaos is gendered female and that the traditional Western figuration of the chaotic feminine as Other may partly explain the rather schizoid nature of chaos science.

8. Baudrillard posits the existence of the hyperreal, a space which is "sheltered from the imaginary, and from any distinction between the real and the imaginary, leaving room only for the orbital recurrence of models and the simulated generation of difference" (1983, 4).

9. Marshall McLuhan makes an interesting distinction between low definition representation, in which "each object [creates] its own space" and an analytic representation, in which "the retinal impression is intensified [and] objects cease to cohere a space of their own making, [becoming] 'contained' in a uniform, continuous, and 'rational' space" (1964, 167). McLuhan's notion of a synthetic, relational definition would seem to anchor the object in a network including other objects as well as the observing subject; an analytic definition would liberate the object from relational texture in a way similar to the effect Baudrillard describes here.

10. McLuhan suggests that literacy leads to visuality, which engages the analytic gaze, which forces the visual field toward fragmentation and repetition (1964, 333); systemic interpretations of texts tend toward a subversion of this reduction and promote a tension between visuality and dynamic process and the maintenance of a part/whole integration. However, under the stress of interpretation and systemic tracking, the object text may alter relations so radically that it breaks down into chaotic turbulence—which may or may not resolve itself into a new order.

11. Hayles suggests that in *Gravity's Rainbow* Pynchon, by refusing to privilege either figure or ground and making both equidistant in his narrative, promotes a gestalt vision. She says this is a conceptualization that makes meaning a "function not of difference but of similarity, arising not from distinguishing parts but from seeing the interconnection of the whole" (1984, 175).

12. Baudrillard suggests that this rigorous procedure is, however, finally unable to define any real position because of its operation within an infinitely small space where on/off may have no value other than registration (1983, 115-16).

13. A fixed or fixable system is a closed one and thus inherently uninteresting under the definition of chaos theory.

14. McLuhan ties fragmentary analytic focus and rampant individuality to the phonetic alphabet, which he describes as inherently visual and distancing. He links the phonetic alphabet to mental structures of lineality, sequence, and cause and effect (1964, 87).

15. Hayles suggests that traditional science, which values simplicity of explanation, resists the new paradigm more vigorously and consistently than literary criticism. She attributes this to the fact that unlike the scientific community, contemporary theorists are driven by an economy of scarcity: texts are continually depleted, their internal resources consumed by literary critics hungry for publication. Hayles notes that poststructuralist theory has converted a closed system of textual canonization and consumption to an open system which accepts even theoretical texts as legitimate sources of literary study; she likens this last to the physical systems which, through autocatalysis, can "spontaneously reorganize themselves at a high level of complexity" (1987, 129).

16. Hayles disagrees with Paulson's extension of Michel Serres's theories into a statement that noise must be "rectified" within all levels of the system; she points out that noise may or may not become useful information, depending upon the "stability of the system, the kind of feed-back loops at work, the amount and kind of noise injected, and when the injection occurs" (1990, 206).

17. Lyotard points out that science is an open system; its capacity for rule and statement generation tends toward a non-denotative form of knowledge, a knowledge that is prescriptive in that it focuses upon the production of rules or admission of moves rather than upon institutionalization of information. He sees this as a recognition of the "heteromorphous" nature of language games and therefore of the necessarily local nature of any form of consensus (1984, 65–66).

18. Hayles notes that Lyotard's valorization of "paralogy" is typical of attempts to see chaos (or local knowledge) as an "antidote to totalization"; these, she says, have a globalizing, universalizing tendency that carries its own danger (1990, 216).

19. Carraway, like Gatsby, conceives of knowledge as a series of lists, not understanding that such a project effaces its subject. Foucault notes that classical taxonomy conceals the organism as it makes visible the "relief of forms, with their elements, their mode of distribution, and their measurements" (1973, 137).

Works Cited

Atlan, Henri. 1979. *Entre le cristal et la fumée: Essai sur l'organisation du vivant*. Paris: Seuil.

Bachelard, Gaston. 1969. *The Poetics of Space*. Translated by Maria Jolas. Boston: Beacon Press.

Bakhtin, Mikhail. 1984. *Rabelais and His World*. Translated by Helene Iswolsky. Bloomington: Indiana University Press.

Barnes, Julian. 1984. *Flaubert's Parrot*. New York: McGraw-Hill.

Barney, Stephen A. 1982. "Chaucer's Lists." In *The Wisdom of Poetry: Essays in Early English Literature in Honor of Morton W. Bloomfield*, edited by Larry D. Benson and Siegfried Wenzel, 189–223. Kalamazoo: Medieval Institute Publications at Western Michigan University.

Barnsley, Michael F., and Stephen G. Demko, eds. 1986. *Chaotic Dynamics and Fractals*. Orlando, Fla.: Academic Press.

Barth, John. 1967. *The Sot-Weed Factor*. Garden City, N.Y.: Doubleday.

———. 1987. *Giles Goat-Boy*. Garden City, N.Y.: Doubleday/Anchor.

———. 1988. *The Floating Opera/The End of the Road*. New York: Doubleday/Anchor.

Barthes, Roland. 1975. *The Pleasure of the Text*. Translated by Richard Miller. New York: Hill and Wang.

Bataille, Georges. 1985. *Visions of Excess*. Minneapolis: University of Minnesota Press.

Bateson, Gregory. 1972. *Steps to an Ecology of Mind*. San Francisco: Chandler.

———. 1979. *Mind and Nature*. New York: Dutton.

Baudrillard, Jean. 1970. "Fetichisme et ideologie: La Reduction semilogique." *Nouvelle Revue de psychanalyse* 2:216–17.

———. 1983. *Simulations*. Translated by Paul Foss, Paul Patton, and Philip Beitchman. New York: Semiotext(e).

Bernheimer, Charles. 1984. "Fetishism and Allegory in *Bouvard et Pecuchet*." In *Flaubert and Postmodernism*, edited by Naomi Schor and Henry F. Majewski, 160–76. Lincoln: University of Nebraska Press.

Bertalanffy, Ludwig von. 1968. *General System Theory*. New York: Braziller.

Borges, Jorge Luis. 1974. "El Idioma Analitico de John Wilkins." In *Obras Completas*, edited by Carlose V. Frias. Buenos Aires: Emece.

Calvino, Italo. 1981. "Myth in the Narrative." In *Surfiction: Fiction Now . . . And Tomorrow*. 2nd ed., edited by Raymond Federman, 75–81. Chicago: Swallow Press.

Campbell, Jeremy. 1982. *Grammatical Man: Information, Entropy, Language, and Life*. New York: Simon & Schuster.

Cooper, Peter L. 1983. *Signs and Symptoms: Thomas Pynchon and the Contemporary World*. Berkeley and Los Angeles: University of California Press.

Crimp, Douglas. 1983. "On the Museum's Ruins." In *The Anti-Aesthetic: Essays on Postmodern Culture*, edited by Hal Foster, 43–56. Port Townsend, Wash.: Bay Press.

DeLillo, Don. 1980. *Ratner's Star*. New York: Random/Vintage.

———. 1985. *White Noise*. New York: Viking.

de Man, Paul. 1984. *The Rhetoric of Romanticism*. New York: Columbia University Press [see Chapter 4, "Autobiography as De-Facement"].

Derrida, Jacques. 1978. *Writing and Difference*. Translated by Alan Bass. Chicago, Ill.: University of Chicago Press.

Donato, Eugenio. 1986. "The Museum's Furnace: Notes toward

a Contextual Reading of *Bouvard and Pécuchet.*" In *Critical Essays on Gustave Flaubert,* edited by Laurence M. Porter, 207–22. Boston: G. K. Hall.

Douglas, Mary. 1972. "Deciphering a Meal." *Daedalus* (Winter): 61-81.

Dretske, Fred I. 1981. *Knowledge & the Flow of Information.* Cambridge, Mass: MIT Press.

Fitzgerald, F. Scott. 1925. *The Great Gatsby.* New York: Scribner's.

———. 1945. *The Crack-Up.* Edited by Edmund Wilson. New York: New Directions.Flaubert, Gustave. 1976. *Bouvard and Pécuchet.* Translated by Alban Krailsheimer. New York: Penguin.

Foucault, Michel. 1972. *The Archaeology of Knowledge.* Translated by A. M. Sheridan Smith. New York: Random/Pantheon.

———. 1973. *The Order of Things: An Archaeology of the Human Sciences.* [No translater listed.] New York: Random/Vintage.

Frampton, Kenneth. 1983. "Toward a Critical Regionalism: Six Points for an Architecture of Resistance." In *The Anti-Aesthetic: Essays on Postmodern Culture,* edited by Hal Foster, 16–30. Port Townsend, Wash: Bay Press.

Gass, William. 1985. "And." In *Voicelust: Eight Contemporary Fiction Writers on Style,* edited by Allen Wier and Don Hendrie, Jr., 101–25. Lincoln: University of Nebraska Press.

Ginsberg, Allen. 1984. "A Supermarket in California." *Collected Poems 1947–1980.* New York: Harper.

Gleick, James. 1987. *Chaos: The Making of a New Science.* New York: Penguin.

Goody, Jack. 1977. *The Domestication of the Savage Mind.* Cambridge, Mass: Cambridge University Press.

Gunn, Janet Varner. 1982. *Autobiography: Toward a Poetics of Experience.* Philadelphia: University of Pennsylvania Press.

Harbison, Robert. 1977. *Eccentric Spaces.* New York: Avon/Hearst.

Hassan, Ihab. 1982. *The Dismemberment of Orpheus: Toward a Postmodern Literature.* Madison: University of Wisconsin Press.

———. 1987. *The Postmodern Turn: Essays in Postmodern Theory and Culture.* Columbus: The Ohio State University Press.

Hayles, N. Katherine. 1984. *The Cosmic Web: Scientific Field Models and Literary Strategies in the Twentieth Century.* Ithaca, N.Y.: Cornell University Press.

Hayles, N. Katherine. 1987. "Information or Noise? Economy of Explanation in Barthes' *S\Z* and Shannon's Information Theory." In *One Culture: Essays in Science and Literature,* edited by George Levine with Alan Rauch, 119–42. Madison: University of Wisconsin Press.

————. 1990. *Chaos Bound: Orderly Disorder in Contemporary Literature and Science.* Ithaca, N.Y.: Cornell University Press.

Henkle, Roger B. 1983. "The Morning and the Evening Funnies: Comedy in *Gravity's Rainbow.*" In *Approaches to Gravity's Rainbow,* edited by Charles Clerc, 272–90. Columbus: The Ohio State University Press.

Hipkiss, Robert A. 1984. *The American Absurd: Pynchon, Vonnegut, and Barth.* Port Washington, N.Y.: Associated University Press.

Hofstadter, Douglas R. 1979. *Gödel, Escher, Bach: An Eternal Golden Braid.* New York: Basic Books.

Hutcheon, Linda. 1980. *Narcissistic Narrative: The Metafictional Paradox.* New York: Methuen.

Jameson, Fredric. 1984. Foreword to *The Postmodern Condition: A Report on Knowledge* by Jean-François Lyotard. Minneapolis: University of Minnesota Press.

Joseph, Gerhard. 1970. *John Barth.* Minneapolis: University of Minnesota Press.

Kenner, Hugh. 1962. *The Stoic Comedians.* Berkeley and Los Angeles: University of California Press.

Kermode, Frank. 1967. *The Sense of an Ending.* London: Oxford University Press.

Lakoff, George. 1987. *Women, Fire, and Dangerous Things: What Categories Reveal about the Mind.* Chicago, Ill.: University of Chicago Press.

Laszlo, Ervin. 1972. *The Systems View of the World: The Natural Philosophy of the New Development in the Sciences.* New York: Braziller.

LeClair, Tom. 1987. *In the Loop: Don DeLillo and the Systems Novel.* Urbana: University of Illinois Press.

Lévi-Strauss, Claude. 1966. *The Savage Mind.* [No translator listed.] Chicago, Ill.: University of Chicago Press.

Lyotard, Jean-François. 1984. *The Postmodern Condition: A Report on Knowledge.* Translated by Geoff Bennington and Brian Massumi. Minneapolis: University of Minnesota Press.

Mandelbrot, Benoit B. 1983. *The Fractal Geometry of Nature*. New York: Freeman.

Maturana, Humberto R. 1978. "Biology of Language: The Epistemology of Reality." In *Psychology and Biology of Language and Thought*, edited by G. Miller and E. Lenneberg. New York: Academic Press.

Mazurek, Raymond A. 1985. "Ideology and Form in Post-Modernist Historical Novels: *The Sot-Weed Factor* and *Gravity's Rainbow*." *Minnesota Review* 25:69–84.

McHale, Brian. 1987. *Postmodernist Fiction*. New York: Methuen.

McLuhan, Marshall. 1964. *Understanding Media: The Extensions of Man*. New York: McGraw-Hill.

Melville, Herman. 1972. *Moby-Dick*. New York: Penguin.

Mendelson, Edward. 1986. "Gravity's Encyclopedia." In *Thomas Pynchon's 'Gravity's Rainbow,'* edited by Harold Bloom, 29–52. New York: Chelsea House.

Miller, Walter M., Jr. 1976. *A Canticle for Liebowitz*. New York: Bantam.

Mooney, Ted. 1981. *Easy Travel to Other Planets*. New York: Ballantine.

Paulson, William R. 1988. *The Noise of Culture: Literary Texts in a World of Information*. Ithaca, N.Y.: Cornell University Press.

Porush, David. 1985. *The Soft Machine: Cybernetic Fiction*. New York: Methuen.

Prigogine, Ilya, and Isabelle Stengers. 1984. *Order Out of Chaos: Man's New Dialogue with Nature*. New York: Bantam.

Pynchon, Thomas. 1973. *Gravity's Rainbow*. New York: Viking/Penguin.

Rabelais, François. 1955. *Gargantua and Pantagruel*. Translated by J. M. Cohen. New York: Penguin.

Resnikoff, Howard L. 1989. *The Illusion of Reality*. New York: Springer.

Ricoeur, Paul. 1965. *History and Truth*. Boston, Mass.: Northeastern University Press.

Safer, Elaine B. 1988. *The Contemporary American Comic Epic: The Novels of Barth, Pynchon, Gaddis, and Kesey*. Detroit, Mich.: Wayne State University Press.

Scarry, Elaine. 1985. *The Body in Pain: The Making and Unmaking of the World*. New York: Oxford University Press.

Scholes, Robert. 1979. *Fabulation and Metafiction.* Urbana: University of Illinois Press.

Schulte-Sasse, Jochen. 1985. "Afterword," "Art and the Sacrifical Structure of Modernity: A Sociohistorical Supplement to Jay Caplan's *Framed Narratives* " in *Framed Narratives: Diderot's Genealogy of the Beholder,* by Jay Caplan, 97–115. Minneapolis: University of Minnesota Press.

Schwab, Gabriele. 1986. "Creative Paranoia and the Frost Patterns of White Words." In *Thomas Pynchon's 'Gravity's Rainbow,'* edited by Harold Bloom, 97–111. New York: Chelsea House.

Seed, David. 1988. *The Fictional Labyrinths of Thomas Pynchon.* Iowa City: University of Iowa Press.

Sorrentino, Gilbert. 1987. *Mulligan Stew.* New York: Grove.

Stark, John O. 1974. *The Literature of Exhaustion: Borges, Nabokov, and Barth.* Durham, N.C.: Duke University Press.

———. 1980. *Pynchon's Fictions: Thomas Pynchon and the Literature of Information.* Athens: Ohio University Press.

Stein, Gertrude. 1962. "Composition as Explanation." In *Selected Writings of Gertrude Stein,* edited by Carl Van Vechten, 511–23. New York: Random/Modern Library.

Stewart, Susan. 1984. *On Longing: Narratives of the Miniature, the Gigantic, the Souvenir, the Collection.* Baltimore, Md.: The Johns Hopkins University Press.

Varela, Francisco. 1979. *Principles of Biological Autonomy.* New York: Elsevier North-Holland.

Vonnegut, Kurt. 1985. *Galapagos.* New York: Dell.

Walkiewicz, E. P. 1986. *John Barth.* Boston: Twayne Publishers.

White, Hayden. 1981. "The Value of Narrativity in the Representation of Reality." In *On Narrative,* edited by W. J. T. Mitchell, 1–23. Chicago, Ill.: University of Chicago Press.

Wiener, Norbert. 1967. *The Human Use of Human Beings: Cybernetics and Society* New York: Avon-Discus.

———. 1968. *Cybernetics.* Cambridge, Mass.: MIT Press.

Wilden, Anthony. 1980. *System and Structure: Essays in Communication and Exchange.* New York: Methuen.

Wittgenstein, Ludwig. 1981. *Tractatus logico-philosophicus.* Translated by C. K. Ogden. London: Routledge.

Wordsworth, William. 1965. "Preface to Second Edition." 1800. In *Lyrical Ballads,* edited by E. L. Brett and A. R. Jones, 241–72. Edinburgh: Constable.

Wurman, Richard Saul. 1988. *Information Anxiety*. Garden City, N.Y.: Doubleday.

Young, Paul. 1987. *The Nature of Information*. New York: Praeger.

Ziegler, Heide. 1987. *John Barth*. New York: Methuen.

Index